"I'll make the land over to your father if you give me a full explanation as to why you left me."

Leonie stared at him blankly. "You're prepared to barter a valuable plot of land just to hear me tell you something you already know?"

"I *don't* know. That's the point." He leaned forward, his eyes locked with hers. "I swear I was never unfaithful while we were together. I loved you, Leonie. And, fool that I am, I thought you loved me."

"I did. You know I did." Her eyes glistened suddenly with unshed tears. "But one day I just happened to be in the wrong place at the wrong time. And my whole life fell apart."

Jonah looked at her in expectant silence, which stretched Leonie's nerves to the limit. "All right, Jonah, I'll explain. But before I start there's something I need to know. You're not the only one after the truth. How many people actually know that Fenny is your daughter?"

A family with a passion for life—and for love.

Welcome to the first book in **The Dysarts**,
a wonderful new series by favorite author
Catherine George. *A Vengeful Reunion* tells the
story of eldest daughter Leonie, who returns
home for a family celebration and finds herself
coming face-to-face with her former fiancé,
Jonah Savage. The handsome property developer
wants to know why she jilted him—even if that
means resorting to a little blackmail and, since
their mutual attraction remains as intense as ever,
getting his revenge!

Over the coming months, you'll get to know each
member of the Dysart family, and share in their
trials and joys, their hopes and dreams, as they live
their lives with passion—and for love.

Look out for Jess's story.
Coming soon in **The Dysarts**

Catherine George

A VENGEFUL REUNION

The Dysarts

HARLEQUIN®

TORONTO • NEW YORK • LONDON
AMSTERDAM • PARIS • SYDNEY • HAMBURG
STOCKHOLM • ATHENS • TOKYO • MILAN • MADRID
PRAGUE • WARSAW • BUDAPEST • AUCKLAND

ISBN 0-373-12166-0

A VENGEFUL REUNION

First North American Publication 2001.

Copyright © 2000 by Catherine George.

Visit us at www.eHarlequin.com

Printed in U.S.A.

CHAPTER ONE

SHE caught the train with seconds to spare. Breathless, she stowed her bag away, sank down into the nearest window seat, shrugged off her overcoat, then sat watching the fields of home rush by as she savoured the surprise she was about to spring.

Once she'd handed over her ticket she got up to head for the buffet car in search of coffee. Several male eyes followed her progress along the swaying carriage, but one pair, more intent than the rest, watched from behind a newspaper, resuming their covert scrutiny as she passed by again on her way back to her seat.

While she drank her coffee she went on with the book she'd started on the plane, and soon became absorbed enough to spare only peripheral attention when the train stopped at Swindon. When someone slid into the seat opposite she shifted her feet out of the way without looking up.

'Good book, Leo?'

Her head flew up as a laconic drawl severed her gaze from the page like a sword-thrust. Stunned, she stared into a lean, black-browed face she had once known only too well. The face was older than at their last meeting, with a few added lines and a new, arresting streak of silver in the ink-dark hair above it. But the high cheekbones and wide, beautifully cut mouth delivered the same, unforgettable impact.

'Well, well, Jonah Savage,' she said at last. 'How are you?'

'At the moment amazed to find myself face to face with the elusive Miss Dysart,' he retorted. 'Something it's been damned difficult to achieve these past few years.'

She smiled politely. 'I still work abroad.'

His brief smile of response stopped short of icy hazel-green eyes. 'So what brings you back?'

'It's Adam's twenty-first today. There's a party at home.'

'I heard you couldn't make it.'

Her eyes narrowed. 'You did? How?'

'I've been spending time at the Pennington office. I've seen your father quite often lately.'

Leonie received the information with hot resentment, and considered moving to another seat. But that would look childish. And there was only an hour to go; even less if Jonah was leaving the train at Bristol Parkway. 'Where are you heading?' she asked.

'Why, Leo?' he drawled. 'Eager to get rid of me?

She shrugged her indifference.

'I'll take that as a no.' His eyes locked onto hers like a heat-seeking missile. 'So. How's life in Florence?'

'Interesting.'

'Are you knee-deep in passionate Italian suitors?'

'No,' she returned coolly. 'Just one.'

He raised a sardonic eyebrow. 'Swept off your feet by Latin charm?'

'Something like that.'

He stood up abruptly. 'I'm off to buy a drink. Can I get you something?'

Leonie refused, then slumped down in her seat in shock as she watched the tall, retreating figure. Jonah

Savage had changed considerably since their last meeting. Which was only to be expected. A lot could happen—*had* happened—in seven years. But the eyes were the same. Like a prowling panther, according to her sister Jess.

'How's business?' she asked, when Jonah returned.

'Very good.' He looked at her analytically. 'How's yours? Do you still enjoy teaching?'

'I do. Very much.'

His wide, expressive mouth curled slightly. 'And what else do you enjoy in Florence, I wonder?'

'Are you being offensive?'

'Not in the least. Just interested.'

Leonie met the relentless eyes with composure. 'My job has expanded over the years. In the day I teach English to Italian children and Italian to little Brits and other expatriate offspring. I supervise games and swimming. And some evenings I give one-to-one English lessons, mainly to businessmen.'

He raised an eyebrow. 'Not much time to spare for your lover.'

Leonie shrugged, refusing to rise. 'My weekends are free, and I teach *some* evenings, not all of them.'

'Is your man in the same profession?'

'No. Roberto's involved in the family business—luxury hotels.'

'Successful?'

'Very. He's the heir apparent. Just like you with your outfit.'

Jonah sipped his coffee, scrutinising her feature by feature. 'You look very different, Leo.'

'Older, you mean.'

'And colder. Or maybe it's just the way you've screwed up your hair.'

She returned the scrutiny. 'You look different, too, Jonah. Harder. And colder, just like me.'

'And what—or who—is responsible for that, I wonder?' he cut back, the eyes narrowed suddenly to a feral
gleam.

Gloves off, thought Leonie, meeting the gleam head-
on. 'It's useless to rehash the past, Jonah.'

'Afraid you might call up old ghosts?' His eyes widened in sudden, stark remorse. 'Hell, Leo, I'm sorry. I
had no intention—'

'I know that!' She changed the subject swiftly, saying
the first thing that came into her head. 'So tell me why
you're travelling my way.'

'The company's bought a property not far from your
place. We're developing the site. I'm camping out there
for a while until I get proper security set up.'

'What house?' said Leonie, frowning. 'There's not
usually much for sale round Stavely.'

'Brockhill,' he informed her.

'I didn't know the Laceys were selling up,' she said,
startled.

'They decided the property was too big for them.'

Leonie felt a sharp pang of regret. 'Their family will
miss the old place. When we were young Jess and I used
to play in the gardens there with Theo and Will Lacey.'
She shivered. 'I'd hate Dad to sell Friars Wood.'

'Why?'

'Because it's my home, of course.'

'You don't spend much time there, Leo.' Cold eyes
held hers. 'And if you marry your Italian home will be
a long way from Friars Wood.'

'That's not the point,' she said tightly. 'The house is
my point of origin. Home to the Dysarts for nearly a
hundred years. I couldn't bear to think of someone else
living there.'

Jonah glanced at his watch and got to his feet. 'Almost

there. I'd better collect my belongings. Goodbye, Leonie.' He gave an oddly formal little bow and strolled back to his seat.

Leonie stared after him, secretly furious that he'd left so abruptly. She should have told Jonah to go the moment she'd laid eyes on him, but now he'd pre-empted her. And called her Leonie, as he'd never done once upon a time. Appalled because she minded so much, she tried to revive her former glow of anticipation. But suddenly she felt tired and travel-weary, and not much in the mood for a party after seeing Jonah again, especially the noisy affair this one was sure to be. Adam had celebrated his actual birthday with fellow students days ago, but tonight they were converging on Friars Wood to celebrate all over again, along with neighbours and friends of the Dysarts. Adam had surprised his parents by requesting a family party for everyone, Leonie had been informed, during her weekly call home from Florence.

At first, bitterly disappointed, Leonie had been sure she couldn't make it. A flu bug had almost halved the teaching staff at the International School, making her absence impossible. But when the epidemic had spread to some of the children the principal had decided to close the school for a while until the epidemic was over. Keeping the glad news secret from her family, Leonie had rushed to buy an airline ticket, kissed Roberto Forli goodbye at Pisa airport and flown home.

When the train was approaching Bristol Parkway Leonie saw Jonah Savage coming towards her along the carriage.

'Is someone meeting you here?' he asked, pausing beside her.

She shook her head, wishing she'd given up the surprise idea and asked her father or Adam to meet her. 'No one knows I'm coming. I'm going on to Newport. I'll get a train from there.'

'My car's parked here, if you'd like a lift,' he said casually. 'I pass your place on the way to Brockhill.'

Her first instinct was to refuse anything at all from Jonah Savage. But the plus of arriving home almost two hours earlier than she'd expected far outweighed the downside of a drive in Jonah's company. 'Thank you,' said Leonie, getting up.

'Not at all,' he said politely, as though they were strangers. 'Let me help you on with your coat.'

As he did so the train gave a sudden lurch, throwing her against him, and for the first time in years Leonie Dysart found herself in Jonah Savage's arms. He released her instantly, poker-faced, took her bag and motioned her ahead of him as the train drew to a halt. Leonie stepped off the train, shivering in the cold February wind, and from rather more than that. She was glad when Jonah set off up the stairs to the footbridge at such a punishing pace it quickly did wonders for both her body heat and her composure as she tried to keep up.

To Leonie's surprise Jonah's car was a well-worn four-wheel drive, very different from the speedy sports models he'd once favoured.

'Practical for your part of the world,' he said laconically, picking up on her thought.

'Very,' she agreed, tensing as Jonah negotiated a busy roundabout with well-remembered panache.

'Don't worry,' he assured her with a sidelong glance. 'I'll get you home in one piece.'

'It just seems strange to be on the left-hand side of the road,' she snapped.

Her oblique reference to life in Italy put an end to conversation as Jonah made for the motorway. But when they reached the Severn Bridge a gusting wind buffeted the car rather ominously as they crossed the river, and Leonie gave a deep, involuntary sigh.

'Still nervous?' asked Jonah, glancing at her.

She smiled. 'Not in the least. The sigh was thanksgiving. Once I'm on the bridge I feel I'm home.'

Jonah's jaw tightened. 'If you're so deeply attached to "home" why stay away so much?'

'You know exactly why,' she said bitterly.

'Now that, Miss Dysart, is where you're wrong. I do not. I have no idea why you ran off and left me, nor the reasons for your self-imposed exile.' He turned a chill, penetrating stare on her for a moment, then returned his attention to the road as he negotiated the descent into Chepstow. 'I got back from New Zealand to read your charming little note ordering me to stay away from you in future. Everything was over between us, you wrote. Unfortunately you omitted a single word of explanation. By that time the funeral was over and you were in Italy, refusing to see me or take my calls, and returning my letters as fast as I posted them. Somehow I could never bring myself to bare my soul in a fax,' he added cuttingly. 'Nor risk the possibility of some Florentine door slammed in my face if I came after you in person.'

'As I said before,' said Leonie coldly, 'it's pointless to rehash the past. Besides,' she added, with sudden heat, 'don't try to play the jilted innocent, Jonah. You know exactly why I—'

'Dumped me?' he said affably.

Leonie glared at him as she pulled a cellphone from

her bag. 'Either stop talking about it or let me out of the car. I can always ring Dad.'

Jonah gave her a searing glance, then drove on in such absolute silence, as she'd requested, that by the end of the journey to Stavely, and home, Leonie was desperate to get out of the car.

'Drop me outside the gates, please,' she said tersely. 'I can walk up to the house.'

He ignored her as they reached the final rise towards Friars Wood, which, like several of its neighbours, was set back from the road in acres of garden and perched high on the cliffs overlooking the Wye Valley. To Leonie's fury Jonah turned in at the gates, driving up the steep, rising bends of the drive to draw up on the terrace in front of the house. The front door immediately flew open, and Adam Dysart hurtled out, grinning from ear to ear as he sprinted down the path and took a flying leap down the steps to pluck his sister from the car into a bear-like hug.

'You made it after all!' he crowed, and whirled her round like a dervish until Leonie begged to be put down, by which time her father and mother were hurrying down to join them. There was a flurry of delighted greetings and kisses as Tom and Frances Dysart welcomed their eldest child home, and, after a swift, incredulous look, behaved as though it were the most natural thing in the world to find Jonah had driven her there.

'Look out!' yelled Adam, as a yellow retriever came streaking up the lawn to hurl itself on Leonie. Jonah's arms shot out to catch her as she tripped, and in the ensuing hubbub any awkwardness was smoothed over as Frances Dysart ordered everyone inside, insisted Jonah came in for a drink, and told her son to go and look for the girls.

'They took Marzi for a walk,' she explained. 'So now they're probably running round in circles, searching for him.'

Leonie hurried inside the house to breathe in the familiar home scents of flowers and cooking and polish, and the occasional whiff of dog. In the kitchen, which had once been two rooms, Frances waved Jonah to a seat with Tom at the oak table the family used for informal meals, then took Leonie with her to the business end of the room. She filled a kettle, put cakes on a plate and took cookies from a tin as she exclaimed over her daughter's surprise appearance.

Leonie leaned against the central island, aware of Jonah talking quietly to her father on the far side of the room as she explained about the flu bug and its unexpected bonus, and how she'd met Jonah by accident on the train and accepted a lift from him.

Frances Dysart gave her a searching look, but made no comment. 'I'm sorry for the flu victims, but it's so good to see you, darling. Roberto couldn't come with you?' she added in an undertone, pouring tea.

'No, too busy,' said Leonie guiltily, fondling the excited dog. The idea of suave, sophisticated Roberto Forli at a party with carousing undergraduates had been so unimaginable she hadn't invited him. 'Besides, there wouldn't have been room to put him up if Adam's crowd are staying the night.'

'We would have managed,' her mother assured her. 'Take these cakes over to your father and Jonah; I'll bring the tea. Where can those girls have gone?' she added anxiously. 'It's getting late.'

Leonie put the plate on the table in front of the men, then darted to the window. 'Here they come now. Something's wrong.'

Adam was striding across the lawn, carrying a small figure in his arms, with seventeen-year-old Kate hurrying after him, wild dark curls blowing in the wind as she tried to keep up with her brother's long legs.

With her husband and Leonie close behind Frances hurried through the old-fashioned scullery to the kitchen door and threw it wide. 'What's the matter?'

'She fell down and grazed her knee,' said Adam cheerfully, and surrendered his wailing burden to his mother, while Kate flew into the kitchen to hug her sister in elation.

'*Leo*—you came after all. Adam never said a word!'

'Couldn't make myself heard above the din,' said Adam, grinning when the invalid's woeful sobs stopped like magic as she slithered from her mother's arms to hurl herself at Leonie.

'Leo, they said you couldn't come!'

'I couldn't miss Adam's special day!' Leonie hugged the little girl, then knelt in front of her, swabbing at her face with a tissue. 'Now then, Fenny, what's all the crying about?'

'I hurt my *knee*, and it's *bleeding*, and it'll show at the *party*.' The blotched, elfin face lit up with a sudden beam. 'Guess what, Leo! I can stay up—'

'For a little while,' warned Frances.

'And only if you stop crying right away,' said Tom Dysart indulgently. 'Come on, sweetheart, let's wash that knee and see the damage.'

But the invalid had finally noticed the visitor, and shot across the room in delight.

'Jonah, you came early!' shrieked Fenny rapturously. 'Will you dance with me tonight?'

'Of course I will,' he promised, smiling at her.

Leonie stared, narrow-eyed, then gave her family a

look which threatened questions later. 'Come on, darling,' she coaxed, detaching Fenny from Jonah. 'Let Dad see to your knee.'

When the knee had been washed, anointed, and a plaster applied, the six-year-old charmer promptly settled herself beside Jonah at the table to eat cake and drink milk, going into great detail as she described her party dress. Leonie shot a resentful glare at Jonah as he listened to the little girl, then turned away to talk to Kate, who was watching her apprehensively, plainly on edge about the entire situation.

'So when's Jess arriving, Kate?'

'She's driving down—should be here any time. You're sharing Fenny's room with Jess and me tonight. Leo, shall I unpack for you?' said Kate, in sudden inspiration. 'Mother, is there anything else you want me to do?'

'Not at the moment.' Frances smiled. 'Afterwards, why don't you have your bath, darling?'

Kate agreed with alacrity, and shot off at such speed Leonie exchanged a wry glance with her mother. 'Desperate to escape.'

'You know Kate can't bear scenes of any kind.'

Leonie frowned. 'And she was worried I might make one?'

'From the look on your face it seemed a distinct possibility, darling!' Frances cast a look towards the little girl sitting among the men like a queen bee. 'I'd better break that up, or she'll get over-excited. Fenny's been looking forward to the party for weeks.'

'She's obviously a great fan of Jonah's—*and* vice versa.'

'Since he's been involved with Brockhill he's been

here a few times lately.' Frances gave her daughter a searching look. 'Do you mind?'

'I'm not entitled to mind.' Leonie smiled a little. 'Fenny's obviously expecting to see Jonah at the party, but don't worry. I promise to behave.'

'When we asked him we thought you wouldn't be here, Leo. As it is we can hardly withdraw the invitation. Besides, it's a long, long time since you broke up with Jonah,' her mother added gently.

'True.' But not long enough to accept his presence in her home with the ease the rest of her family felt, particularly Adam, who was laughing his head off at something Jonah had just told him. Leonie felt oddly left out. And as though he sensed it Jonah caught her eye and got to his feet.

'Time I was off,' he said quickly. 'Thank you for the tea, Mrs Dysart.'

'Thank *you* for bringing Leonie home,' said Tom. 'We'll expect you back later. Might be a good idea to come on foot if the weather holds, Jonah, to avoid parking problems.'

Adam looked at his watch and whistled. 'I'd better get off down to Chepstow to meet some people off the train.'

'I've put containers of sandwiches in your fridge for a snack,' said his mother, 'so you can all congregate there to start with while Leo helps me set out the food in the dining room. The boys can get ready in your place, too, but the girls come in here to dress once you've fed them.'

'Yes, ma'am,' said her son, saluting smartly. 'See you later, Jonah.'

'Come on, Fenny,' said Frances, 'bathtime. You can have supper in front of the TV in the study.'

'I might spoil my party frock,' protested Fenny.

'Dressing gown until the guests arrive, and change into your frock at the last minute,' said Frances firmly.

Fenny blew a kiss to Jonah, gave Leonie a big hug, patted the dog, then skipped from the room with her mother, chattering excitedly.

'See Jonah to the door, Leonie,' said her father briskly. 'I'm going to walk the dog down to the farm. He's staying there overnight, out of the way.'

'You don't have to see me out, Leo,' said Jonah when they were alone. 'Though I'm glad of a moment in private. I was told you wouldn't be here today. Otherwise I would have refused the invitation.'

She eyed him challengingly. 'To avoid meeting up with me again?'

His mouth tightened. 'To save you the misfortune of meeting up with *me* again.'

'Since we've already done that it doesn't really matter, does it?' Leonie walked along the hall with him and opened the front door. 'So for pity's sake turn up tonight, Jonah, otherwise Mother—still a great fan of yours, by the way—will think I was so rude I put you off.'

'Put like that, how can I refuse?' he said dryly.

Leonie gazed out over the descending tiers of the garden, barely visible now in the twilight. 'Besides,' she said casually, 'if you stayed away it would very obviously spoil Fenny's evening. Which comes as rather a surprise. I know about the presents at Christmas and birthdays, and so on, but I had no idea she knew you so well in person.'

Jonah leaned against the arch of the porch, his eyes on her face. 'When your parents heard I was developing Brockhill for the company they asked me to drop in whenever I'm in Stavely.'

'So you're a regular visitor?'

'Only when I'm invited,' he assured her.

She shrugged. 'I suppose I shouldn't be surprised. The entire family was upset when we broke up.'

'You mean when you jilted me.'

'Can you blame me?' she said bitterly.

'Damn right I do,' he snapped. 'You condemned me without trial.'

'I had good reason!'

'If this reason of yours was so good, why did you refuse to share it with me?' he demanded with sudden savagery. 'Or even with your parents?'

Leonie looked up into eyes that were no longer icy, but glowing with a look of such molten anger she backed away, her retreat cut off by the door he pulled closed behind her.

'Now you're out in the cold, just like me.' He seized her wrists. 'How does it feel, Leo?'

'Let me go, Jonah,' she ordered, teeth gritted.

'Not until I get something straight. God knows if I'll ever get the opportunity again.' His eyes bored into hers. 'You owe me an explanation, Leo.'

'You mean it still matters to you, after all these years?' she said scornfully. 'I don't believe it.'

The grip on her wrists tightened. 'Whether you believe it or not, Leo, I want the truth at last.'

Leonie glared at him impotently, trying to free herself, but salvation appeared in the form of cars which came roaring up the drive with blaring horns and flashing headlights. Two of the cars turned off to the stable block, the other streaked along the terrace past Jonah's car, and came to a showy stop in a spurt of gravel under the bare branches of the chestnut tree by the summerhouse.

'The cavalry,' drawled Jonah, and released her.

Jessamy Dysart leapt from her car and gave a screech of pleasure as she saw her sister. Leonie ran down to throw her arms round her and Jess hugged her in return, exclaiming over the surprise.

'I thought you couldn't make it, Leo—fantastic!' She peered up at the man coming down the steps towards them in the half-light. 'Is this the famous Roberto I've been hearing about—?' She stopped short, her dark eyes like saucers. *'Jonah?'*

'He's just going,' said Leonie swiftly.

'Hello, Jess.' Jonah stretched out a hand and Jess took it, looking from him to Leonie in frank speculation. 'And goodbye,' he added dryly. 'I'll see you later.'

'You're coming to the party?' said Jess incredulously.

'Wouldn't miss it for the world,' he assured her. 'I've promised to dance with a certain lady—wouldn't do to disappoint her.'

Leonie shook her head in response to Jess's look of wild enquiry. 'He means Fenny.'

Jonah gave them a mocking bow, got in his car and backed along the terrace, pausing to allow another vehicle to turn off to the stable block before he drove out of sight down the winding drive.

'I've obviously missed a bit somewhere,' said Jess, looking stunned as they went up to the house. 'Since when were you and Jonah Savage on speaking terms again?'

'We're not,' said Leonie tersely, and explained the encounter on the train. 'Did you know he's been coming to Friars Wood lately?'

'No, I didn't. I haven't been home for a while.' Jess grinned sheepishly. 'Busy social life.'

'You don't say!' said Leonie dryly. 'Come on, get the hugs and kisses over, then Mother requires help.

Afterwards we'll grab Kate and put in an appearance at the Stables as official welcome party.'

Before they went inside Jess gave her sister a searching look. 'Do you mind, Leo? That Jonah's coming tonight?'

'Not in the least.'

'Liar!'

Leonie grinned. 'All right, I do mind. But no one will know, I promise. Especially Jonah Savage.'

CHAPTER TWO

FRIARS WOOD had been built a century earlier on the site of a mediaeval chantry chapel where masses had once been sung for the souls of the departed. Of no particular architectural category, it was a house of great charm, with groups of chimneys with barley-sugar twists, and a great many small-paned windows. At the front a verandah formed a balcony for the upper floor, with a wrought-iron pillar giving support to the ancient wistaria which wreathed verandah and balcony in clusters of purple blossom twice a year.

When Tom and Frances Dysart had taken over Friars Wood, after they'd married, Tom's parents had moved into the converted stable block, which they'd shared with his young sister Rachel. It was an arrangement which had worked well as the head count of young Dysarts mounted in the main house. Years later, when both senior Dysarts had died within a short time of each other, and Rachel had long been established in a career and home of her own in London, the Stables had been used as a guest house for visitors, until Adam's eighteenth birthday, when it had been handed over to him for his own personal retreat.

In the still cold of this particular night the Stables were a very animated place, blazing with light in every room and with Adam's guests crammed into every corner as they tucked into the snacks provided to tide them over until the buffet supper later at the main house.

'Come on, Kate,' said Leonie affectionately, as her younger sister hung back as usual as they approached the stable block.

'That's right, love,' said Jess, 'chin up, chest out and *smile*!' She tickled her small sister in the ribs, prodding her forward just as the door flew open and several young men fell back in mock-awe.

'Get yourself out here, Dysart,' yelled one of them, 'I've just seen a vision—in triplicate!'

'It's the three graces,' sighed another reverently.

'Show some respect,' ordered Adam, amiably cuffing them out of the way. 'These are my sisters, Leonie, Jessamy and Katharine, whom you may address, if they grant permission, as Leo, Jess and Kate.'

While Adam rattled off introductions, the exuberant young guests, male and female, crowded round his sisters, pressing them to drinks.

'No alcohol until after supper,' Adam explained, handing orange juice to Leonie.

'Did they go along with that?' she asked in an undertone.

'Absolutely. We had a pretty wild night on my birthday in Edinburgh. But here on my own patch I've laid down the law—no drinking until after supper, and no sneaking back here for illicit snogging and so on. I took them along the cliff path as far as the Eyrie earlier, to warn that it's a good six hundred feet down from the path to the River Wye, and I'll repeat the process when the rest of the gang arrive.' Adam grinned. 'And don't worry about Kate. I'll make sure she has a good time.' He shouted for silence. 'Listen up, you lot, my sisters are taking the women over to the house to change, and allocate bedrooms. I'll introduce the men to my parents later.'

Back at the house time flew by in a flurry of preparation.

Young female guests were shown into the three bed-rooms normally occupied by the daughters of the house, and the stream of traffic was constant along the long upper landing as jeans and sweaters were exchanged for scanty little dresses. Everyone jostled for places at full-length mirrors, and latecomers arrived to join in the me-lee.

'Thank goodness you had a bath earlier on, Kate,' said Leonie in the haven of Fenny's little room. 'Bags first shower, Jess—I feel travel-stained.'

Later the three of them went downstairs to join their parents for a glass of wine in the lull before more guests arrived. Fenny, in pink taffeta and lacy tights, her dark hair caught up with a velvet bow, was incandescent with excitement as she saw her sisters.

'You all look *gorgeous*,' she cried, rushing from one to the other in admiration.

'Fenny's right,' agreed Tom Dysart, smiling proudly on his daughters.

'It's amazing how genetics work,' said Frances with satisfaction. 'You've all got something of your father and me, in various permutations.'

'Only I drew the short straw,' sighed Kate, pulling a face. 'And I do mean *short*.'

'You look stunning,' said Leonie firmly. 'And be thankful. Only someone as small as you could wear a dress like that.'

In brief, mint-green organza, with her hair coaxed up into a loose knot of curls, Kate looked very different from her everyday schoolgirl self, but it had taken naked envy from some of Adam's girlfriends to convince her of the fact.

Leonie had released her own hair from its severe braided coil to cascade in bronze glory to her shoulders, and wore a scarlet silk sheath of such superb cut Jess eyed it reverently.

'I admire your style, chancing that colour with *your* hair. Must have cost a lira or two,' she muttered.

'You didn't pick that little number up in a charity shop, either,' retorted Leonie. 'Looks as though you were shrink-wrapped into it.'

Jess grinned. 'I knew Adam's girlies would all be wearing floaty little numbers so I opted for black and sexy.'

'Very different from Leonie's twenty-first,' said their mother reminiscently. 'That was all satin ballgowns.'

'Except for Leo,' said Jess bitterly. 'She conned you into buying her that clinging gold job with the plunging back. It made the rest of us look like lampshades.'

'I wasn't even allowed to stay up,' said Kate, smiling at Fenny. 'You're a lucky girl.'

'I know,' said Fenny, pink with excitement. '*And* I'm going to sleep on the folding bed in Mummy's room.'

There was sudden commotion as the male contingent arrived from the stables; the girls stampeded down the stairs to join them, and Adam's voice, loud above the rest, shouted that some of the neighbours had arrived, along with the DJ and the music equipment.

Tom Dysart hurried off to supervise installation in the conservatory off the dining room, and Frances followed him with Kate and Fenny to welcome the newcomers, but her elder daughters remained behind for a moment of quiet together before the party began in earnest.

'How long are you home for, Leo?' asked Jess.

'Two weeks, at least.' Leonie explained about the flu epidemic.

Jess whistled. 'Won't this Roberto of yours object?'

'He wasn't happy.'

'He'd be even less so if he knew Jonah Savage was on the scene. Or doesn't he know about Jonah?'

'No. Though it wouldn't matter if he did.' Leonie shrugged. 'I'm nearly thirty, Jess. It would be pretty strange if I hadn't had a boyfriend or two in the past.'

Jess gave her a scathing look. 'Come off it, Leo. You and Jonah were crazy about each other.'

'But not any more. Come on. Time we joined the fray.'

'In a minute.' Jess put a hand on her arm. 'Look, I wouldn't bring this up if Jonah hadn't reappeared on the scene, but come on, Leo, after all this time surely you can tell me what happened. Please. I promise I'll never mention it again.'

'The usual thing. I found out he was involved with someone else.' Leonie's mouth curved in a wry, bitter smile. 'And so, dear reader, I bolted back to Italy, and instead of coming home at the end of the academic year to get married, I stayed on at the school to become Miss Jean Brodie, Italian-style.'

Jess whistled softly. 'I knew it had to be something like that, but I just couldn't believe it. And don't worry. I won't tell anyone.'

'You'd better not. Everyone else—including Mother and Dad—thinks I just changed my mind,' warned Leonie.

'Except Jonah, of course.'

'Including Jonah. He never knew I found out.'

'*What?*' Jess frowned. 'Who was the woman, Leo?'

'Not my secret to tell.'

'Whoever it was, the affair died a quick death— what's the matter?'

'Indigestion.'

'You know my boss is a friend of his,' Jess went on.

'Plenty of female company in Jonah's life, I hear, but nothing permanent. Is Roberto permanent?' she added.

'I think he wants to be.'

'And what do you want—or need?'

Leonie smiled brightly. 'At this moment in time, entertainment. Let's party.'

The drawing room was soon thronged with friends and neighbours, but the younger set crammed into the vast dining room, where the ancient Persian carpet had been taken up to leave the gleaming wood floor bare for dancing. The chairs had been removed, and the dining table pushed against one wall and laden with the supper Frances Dysart had decreed should be eaten the moment all the guests had arrived, before there was any dancing or too much consumption of the wine and beer provided.

'I want your friends to line their stomachs first,' Frances told her son very firmly.

When Jonah Savage was shown in Leonie was describing her life in Florence to some of her parents' friends. She felt Kate stiffen with apprehension beside her, but Fenny charged across the room, her face aglow, and before Jonah could do more than murmur a conventional greeting the little girl had towed him to the far side of the room to join the group round her parents. Leonie saw him shake his head, smiling, as her mother offered him supper, then turned her attention back to the Andersons, who had known her all her life, and were doing their level best to behave as though they'd never received an invitation to the wedding of Leonie Dysart and Jonah Savage.

Sheer will-power forced Leonie to carry on eating, talking and behaving as though the arrival of her one-time fiancé was of no more note than any other guest. But sensitive Kate promptly rescued Leonie's abandoned

supper, and roped her into taking trays of plates off to
the kitchen, where Mrs Briggs, who helped in the house
on weekdays, was firmly in charge, with the help of one
of her daughters. Leonie spent a few minutes chatting
with them in the kitchen, then took Kate by the arm.

'Right then, love,' she said firmly. 'Time for you to
join the younger set.'

Kate looked at her in entreaty. 'I can't go in there on
my own—'

'You don't have to. I'll come with you.'

As Adam had promised, Kate was instantly absorbed
into a crowd of friendly young people, and Leonie, wanting nothing more than a bed to herself in the dark, returned to the drawing room to help Jess circulate with
wine.

Jonah Savage was talking to some of her father's
friends as Leonie and Jess removed plates, and refilled
glasses.

'Are you sure I can't get you anything to eat, Jonah,'
asked Leonie, smiling brightly as she poured more wine
into his glass.

Before he could reply a great thumping beat began to
reverberate through the room, and Fenny let out a
screech of excitement.

'It's the disco, Mummy. *Please* can I go in the party
now?'

'I'll take her, if I may,' Jonah offered.

Frances nodded and Jonah bowed formally to the ecstatic six-year-old.

'May I have this dance, Miss Dysart?'

Tom Dysart grinned ruefully at the assembled guests,
and suggested that everyone join the party to hop around
to the noise for a few minutes. 'Afterwards,' he

added, 'we'll leave the energetic bit to the young and get back here for coffee and medicinal brandy.'

The moment Leonie and Jess joined the dancers they were drawn into the throng, where Kate was dancing happily with one of Adam's friends, showing no trace of her earlier shyness. For a breathless few minutes the older set valiantly kept pace with the young, then Adam had a word with the disc jockey and turned to grin at his parents as Frank Sinatra began to sing 'My Funny Valentine'.

Frances Dysart, née Valentine, blew her son a kiss, and Adam scooped Fenny up and settled the beaming little girl on his hip as he jigged slowly round with total disregard for timing.

'Mind if I cut in?' said Jonah, and Leonie's partner, unversed in the skills of ballroom dancing, surrendered her to him with a rueful grin.

In Jonah's arms Leonie moved in silence to the music, her body in instant, perfect rhythm with his, as it had always been in the past, both on the dance floor and in private. Jonah held her lightly enough, but the touch of his hand on her back burned through the silk of her dress. She tensed, certain that everyone must be watching and speculating, felt his fingers tighten on her hand, and at last surrendered to the eyes that were willing her to look up.

'It's been a long time,' said Jonah softly, and pulled her closer. Her heart leapt as she felt his body stir against her. She tried to put space between them, but his hand hardened against her back, keeping her in contact so close her face flamed, and her dress felt suddenly too tight as her breasts hardened in response impossible to control. She stared blindly over his shoulder, trying to ignore the heat which penetrated through their clothes, her gossamer silk and the fine Italian wool of Jonah's suit no barrier to the desire that surged between them like an electric current.

Then the music stopped and Jonah released her, smiling at her in narrow-eyed triumph. He thanked her with impeccable courtesy, then to Leonie's secret rage deserted her to partner Jess.

Leonie left them to it, and went upstairs to Fenny's room for a few private moments of recovery and repair. Afterwards she went to help serve coffee and drinks in the drawing room, and stayed there, chatting for a while, until her mother asked if she felt brave enough to detach Fenella from the party.

'You know she'll do anything for you, Leo, but be firm,' said Tom Dysart, puffing on a large cigar.

'Don't worry,' Leonie assured him. 'She's probably worn out by now.'

Fenny was tired enough, but tearfully reluctant to leave the revels. She clung to Jonah's hand, pleading to stay a little longer.

'Darling, it's very late,' said Leonie gently. 'Say goodnight to everyone, there's a love.'

Adam solved the problem by stopping the music. He ordered everyone to bid farewell to Miss Fenella Dysart, and after a chorus of goodnights and blown kisses Fenny allowed Jonah to lead her from the room.

'Will you come up and read to me, Jonah? Please?' she cajoled.

He smiled at her indulgently. 'I'm told you can read very well yourself.'

'I'm too tired,' said Fenny, sounding so forlorn Leonie relented.

'I'll take you along to Mother and Dad to say goodnight very quickly to everyone, and when you're tucked up in bed perhaps Jonah would be kind enough to read a very short story?' she said, casting a look at him.

'With pleasure,' he said promptly.

In her parents' rather draughty bathroom later, Leonie hurried the drooping little girl through her preparations for bed, then settled her down on the folding bed in the dressing room off the main bedroom, and went out onto the landing to beckon Jonah inside.

It was a painful, disturbing experience to listen while Jonah read to Fenny. Watching, Leonie felt a sharp, agonising pang for what might have been; survived it, then, when Fenny was asleep, went ahead of Jonah through her parents' room and out onto the landing.

'Thank you,' she said formally. 'If you'd like to go downstairs to join whichever company you prefer, I'll be down in a few minutes. I need repairs.'

'I'll wait here for you.'

'Please don't,' she said coldly.

His eyes narrowed. 'Ah. Back to square one again.'

'What did you expect?'

'Are you telling me I imagined what happened when we were dancing?' he demanded fiercely.

'No,' she snapped. 'I'm not. We were always very—compatible in that way. But you can't use sex like a dose of antibiotics, Jonah. Some things it can't cure.'

'Sex,' he repeated, after a taut, throbbing silence. 'How succinct. A shame you're not equally so on other subjects. Our broken engagement, for instance.'

'Hypocrite! You *know*—' She turned away abruptly as a group of girls came streaming up the stairs in search of a bathroom. 'See you later,' she added out loud, and gave him a fever-bright smile of dismissal.

A peep in at the dancers later showed Adam, Jess and Kate quite literally having a ball, but Leonie, feeling a hundred years older than her siblings, made no move to join them. She returned to the less frenetic atmosphere of the drawing room instead, and circulated among the company, topping up drinks, stopping to chat here and there. And she took good care to extend her civility and her smile in equal measures to Jonah when he came in, knowing full well that everyone in the room was speculating on his presence and her reaction to it. When her parents' guests began to leave at last Leonie seized on the job of escorting them out, and eventually found herself alone at the door with Jonah.

'Say my goodnights to Adam and your sisters,' he said coolly.

'You've given up dancing already?'

His eyes shuttered. 'I've given up a lot of things, Leo. Hope included.'

Leonie shivered in the open doorway in the icy wind blowing up from the river. 'I'm sorry to hear that,' she said politely.

'Are you?' He shrugged. 'You know, Leo, for a moment, as I held you in my arms, I was fool enough to hope things had changed.'

'Nothing's changed,' she said with sudden passion. 'How you can act the innocent, Jonah, when all the time—' She broke off, suddenly weary. 'Oh what's the use? You and I both know what happened. Why do you think I stay away from home so much?'

'I wish I knew,' he retorted. 'Enlighten me.'

She stared at him, shaking her head. 'What a marvellous actor you are, Jonah Savage. You're so brilliant in the role of wronged fiancé—' Leonie smiled brightly as her parents escorted the last of their guests along the hall towards them. 'Thank you so much for sparing the time tonight, Jonah,' she said distinctly. 'You made Fenny very happy.'

'I'm glad,' he responded in kind. 'She's a delightful little girl.' He turned to smile at Tom and Frances Dysart. 'It was a great party. Thank you for inviting me.'

Jonah departed with the Andersons, after general farewells that required nothing more of Leonie than the smile which felt pasted to her face. Afterwards she told her parents she was too tired to rejoin the dancing.

'You won't get much sleep,' said her mother ruefully. 'I'm afraid the music won't stop until two at the earliest.'

'Never mind.' Leonie eyed her spike-heeled scarlet sandals with hostility. 'At least I can take these off!'

Later, huddled under a quilt on the inflated mattress set up beside Fenny's double bed, Leonie knew that even if the house were perfectly quiet she would still be awake. Seeing Jonah again, and, worse still, discovering that the old, familiar chemistry was as strong as ever, was no recipe for sleep. Seven long years, she thought bitterly, yet the pain still cut like a knife. When she'd posted Jonah's ring to him and fled back to Italy that fateful spring her astounded parents had taken a lot of convincing before accepting her repeated explanation about changing her mind. They had taken to Jonah from the first. And very obviously still looked on him as the injured party. She gritted her teeth in frustration. Now he was in the neighbourhood, it was an impossible situation. And because everyone knew the school was closed she could hardly hurt her parents by running back to Florence again to keep out of the way. Nor would she. Jonah couldn't be allowed the satisfaction of spoiling her unexpected holiday.

'Are you awake?' whispered Jess, closing the door quietly.

'You have to be joking!' Leonie switched on a lamp and sat up, eyeing the tray Jess put down beside her. 'Do I smell hot chocolate?'

'You certainly do. I'm a star,' said Jess, handing her a steaming mug. 'I take it I share with Kate? Good thing she's so small.' She sat down on the edge of the bed with a yawn, then sipped with relish. 'I hope this sits well with champagne.'

'So do I. If you get up in the night don't wake me!'

'Do you boss Roberto round like that?'

Leonie smiled demurely. 'No. He's the masterful type.'

Jess stared. 'Really? Does that turn you on?'

'A bit, I suppose.'

'Personally,' said Jess, grinning, 'I think this Roberto of yours must be really something if he outdoes Jonah in the turning-on department.'

'That was a long time ago,' said Leonie dismissively.

'Who are you trying to kid?' Jess's dark eyes mocked beneath the ash-blonde hair. 'I saw you earlier on tonight.'

Leonie felt heat rush to her face. 'You could see?'

'Only because I was just behind you. No one else noticed, Leo. But from where I was standing—shuffling about, really; the boy couldn't dance—it was pretty steamy.'

Leonie groaned and laid her head down on her knees. 'Jonah was making an experiment to prove something to me. And it worked, damn him.'

'Chemistry lesson?'

'Exactly.'

Jess sighed. 'No wonder you looked a bit hacked off when he asked me to dance.' She grinned. 'Not that I was flattered. I just happened to be nearest. He never said a solitary word except to thank me politely afterwards and take off as soon as he could.'

Leonie raised her head again, her eyes heavy. 'It was so mortifying, Jess. The hormones still responded to Jonah no matter how hard the brain tried to put on the brakes.' She shrugged. 'Not that it matters. I'm unlikely to see him again.'

Jess frowned. 'But if you still feel like that after all these years, Leo, couldn't you bring yourself to forgive Jonah's one indiscretion and get together again? I assume it was just the one?' she added.

'As far as I know. But don't be fooled by what happened tonight, there's absolutely no chance of my getting back with Jonah. Ever.'

'Pity.' Jess sighed, then stood up to wriggle out of her dress. 'Though that's tempting fate a bit, Leo. Never say never.'

CHAPTER THREE

NEXT morning, after what felt like only a few minutes' sleep, Leonie got up early to help her mother provide breakfast for any of the guests who could face it. She slid out of bed as quietly as she could to let Jess and Kate sleep on, washed and dressed in Fenny's little bathroom and went downstairs in the pale light of a cool spring morning.

Glad to find the kitchen empty, and her parents and Fenny still presumably sleeping, Leonie laid the big table, set out an array of cups and beakers on the central island, then filled kettles and got out coffee, sliced bread. Afterwards she made herself a pot of tea and some toast, surprised to find she was hungry. When her mother arrived a little later she smiled in surprise.

'You're early, darling, I hoped you'd sleep in for a bit.'

'I opted for the inflatable mattress,' said Leonie, grinning. 'It was no hardship to desert it for the lures of breakfast.' She poured tea for her mother, and offered to make toast.

'Thank you, I think I will. Frankly I could have stayed in bed a lot longer this morning, but I had visions of pallid, hungover young things needing coffee and no one here to provide it.'

'They could have gone over to the Stables and made Adam feed them.'

'Always supposing they could wake him.' Frances

laughed. 'I wonder how everyone slept? I imagine there was quite a fight for beds.'

'Students are used to sleeping on floors,' Leonie assured her. 'I did it often enough in my youth.'

'Darling, you talk as though you were Methuselah!'

'I'm staring thirty in the face, Mother,' Leonie reminded her.

'You don't look it this morning in those jeans. And last night you positively dazzled in that amazing dress. Nor was I the only one to think so.' Frances buttered her toast and bit into it appreciatively. 'I needed this. I didn't eat much last night. And you abandoned *your* supper the moment Jonah arrived.'

Leonie eyed her mother in amusement. 'Nothing gets by you, does it?'

The interlude of peace was short. In twos and threes the yawning party goers came down to join them. When Tom Dysart arrived with Fenny and Kate he gave a wry look into the room full of chattering females, and accepted with alacrity when offered a tray in his study.

Leonie took it in to him with the Sunday papers, stayed to chat for a while, then volunteered to fetch Marzi from the farm while Fenny and Kate had breakfast with the other girls. She collected a jacket from a peg in the scullery and went out alone into the crisp, bright morning, her lips twitching at the sight of drawn curtains and total absence of life in the Stables.

Leonie walked briskly down the drive and out on to the main road, passing only the occasional churchgoing car in the quiet of early Sunday. After a mile or so she turned down the lane which led to Springfield Farm, smiling at the sounds of yapping and barking in the distance as pungent, familiar smells came up to greet her. When she reached the farmhouse a young giant in stockinged feet opened the door in answer to her knock, Chris Morgan's yawn changing to a grin at the sight of his visitor.

'Well, well, Leo Dysart, home from foreign parts! Come in, come in.'

'Hi, Chris, nice to see you again.'

Leonie kicked off her muddy boots in the back entry and followed Chris into the welcoming warmth of a kitchen where tempting smells of fried bacon hung in the air. Chris gestured towards the table and pushed the teapot towards her.

'Sit down, help yourself. My father's taken your dog out with ours. They'll be back in a minute. My mother's away, visiting my sister and new sprog.'

Leonie exclaimed in surprise. She'd attended primary school with both Chris and his sister Jenny. It came as a shock to hear that the new 'sprog' was Jenny's third son.

Chris was all for providing Leonie with a vast fry-up, like the one he was devouring himself, but she shook her head, laughing.

'I've had breakfast. And if I ate one like that every morning I'd need a new wardrobe.'

He grinned. 'My turn for the milking this morning, I need refuelling. Besides, I'm a growing lad.'

'Heavens, I hope not!'

'How did the party go?' he asked, as he went on with his meal.

'Very well. I've left Mother and Kate serving coffee to the female revellers. There was no sign of life from Adam's place.'

Chris made himself a sandwich with the last of his bacon and sat back, looking at her with open pleasure.

'You look very perky for the morning after, Leo. Downright gorgeous, in fact.'

'Why, thank you, kind sir,' she retorted, fluttering her eyelashes. 'Though if I do it's a wonder. I spent half of yesterday travelling, and the other half partying. I'll probably collapse in a heap today at some stage.'

Chris got up, eyebrows raised, in response to a knock on the back door. 'Like Piccadilly Circus here this morning,' he said, grinning.

The grin was missing when he returned with the new arrival.

'Hello, Leo, I didn't know you were here,' said Jonah briskly. 'I've come to collect the shotgun Denzil promised me.'

After years of never laying eyes on Jonah Savage, Leonie could hardly believe she was in his company for the third time in less than twenty-four hours.

'Good morning,' she said frostily.

Chris gestured towards the teapot. 'Like a cup, Jonah? My father's out with the dogs; he won't be long.'

'No hurry. No tea, either, thanks.'

There was an awkward pause while Jonah surveyed the easy familiarity of the scene with a look which set Leonie's teeth on edge.

Chris cleared his throat awkwardly. 'I'll just go out and look for Dad,' he announced, and took himself off with such obvious relief Jonah raised a supercilious eyebrow.

'I trust I didn't interrupt anything.'

Leonie shrugged. 'I was just telling Chris about the party.'

'I see. Did you enjoy it?'

'Yes, very much. Did you?'

Jonah sat down in Chris's chair. 'No, Leo, I did not.

In fact, once I knew you were home after all I was tempted to invent something life-threatening and stay away.'

'But of course you couldn't disappoint Fenny.'

'Exactly.' He eyed her searchingly. 'Leo, every time you mention the child you get that Medusa-like look on your face. Don't you *like* Fenny?'

'How dare you say that? I adore Fenny. But because of you I never see enough of her. And then I come home to find she only has eyes for you—' She lapsed into silence, furious with herself.

Jonah smiled mockingly. 'Jealous?'

Leonie's heated reply was cut off by the arrival of Denzil and Chris Morgan, with a very muddy, excited retriever who greeted her with exuberance. She thanked the Morgans, clipped on Marzi's lead, refused Jonah's offer of a lift, and went outside to chat with Chris in the yard for a minute or two before starting off for home.

Steaming up the steep hill from the farm, with a panting Marzi at her side, Leonie had worked off some of her anger by the time a familiar car drew level.

'Sure you don't want a lift?' asked Jonah through the car window.

Leonie gave him a honeyed smile. 'Certain, thanks. I'm enjoying the walk—and my own company.'

'Then I'll leave you to it.' Jonah nodded coolly, and drove off.

When Leonie reached the gates of Friars Wood she unfastened Marzi's leash, then stopped off at the Stables, to find Adam's friends packing themselves into various cars for the journey to the station, or the trip to Edinburgh, with Fenny and Kate in attendance.

Leonie was greeted with enthusiasm, and though some of the faces were ominously pale everyone reiterated vociferous thanks for the wonderful party. There were kisses all round, and hugs for Fenny, then the convoy of cars began to move down the drive.

'When are *you* going back?' asked Leonie, taking Fenny's hand to walk back to the house with Adam and Kate.

'After Mother's Sunday lunch, of course,' said Adam, who stood three inches over six feet and had an appetite which belied his lanky frame.

'We ought to be eating leftovers from last night,' said Kate, giving him a teasing smile, 'but Mother's roasting beef and whipping up gallons of Yorkshire pudding batter for her darling son as we speak.'

'Yummy,' said Fenny, her hand in Leonie's. 'It's my favourite. Do you have it in Italy, Leo?'

'Not really, no.' Leonie smiled down into the small, shining face. 'But I eat lots of other delicious things.'

'Is Jonah coming to lunch?'

Leonie devoutly hoped not. 'I don't think so, darling. Let's go and help Mother.'

'And wake Jess,' said Adam with relish. 'And don't worry about the party leftovers—I'll take any surplus back with me.'

'As usual,' taunted Kate, then shrieked as Adam made a dive for her, slung her over his shoulder like a sack of potatoes and ran with her through the scullery into the kitchen, Fenny and Leonie laughing as they followed them in.

'*Please!*' implored Jess, holding a hand to her head. 'Less noise, children, for pity's sake.'

'Too much champagne?' enquired Adam as he set Kate down.

'Too much music,' groaned Jess. 'I can still hear that thumping.'

'Have some more tea,' advised her mother, 'then it's all hands on deck, please. Adam wants to be away in reasonable time.'

To Leonie it was a pleasure all the more acute for being so rare as she sat down to family Sunday lunch. Despite the run-in with Jonah, her walk had given her an appetite, and during the meal she entertained a rapt Fenny with tales of the little girls she taught in Florence.

'Can't you come home and teach little girls here, Leo?' pleaded Fenny.

'One day, perhaps,' said Leonie brightly.

There was a brief, awkward silence, then Jess plunged into a humorous anecdote about her flatmate in London. After the pudding plates were cleared away, and Fenny had been allowed to watch a cartoon video in the study, they were drinking coffee when Tom Dysart told his family that there was more to this family lunch than usual.

'Now that I've got you all together for once,' said her father, after exchanging a glance with his wife, 'I think I should tell you I've had an offer for Friars Wood.'

There was dead silence for a moment, as several pairs of eyes stared at him in utter consternation.

Leonie was the first to recover. 'You're not serious, Dad!'

Her father smiled at her wryly. 'I don't joke about Friars Wood, my love.'

'Who the devil wants to buy it?' demanded Adam, incensed.

'That isn't important for the moment,' said Tom Dysart. 'The point is, how do you all feel about it? Discounting the offer—which is staggeringly generous—you must face the fact that one day your mother and I will no longer be here.'

'Daddy, don't!' said Kate, her eyes filling with tears. 'I can't bear it when you talk like that.'

Jess squeezed her hand, and turned anxious eyes on her father. 'Are you short of money, Dad? You're not ill or anything, are you?' she added in sudden alarm.

'No, nothing like that,' said Frances quickly. 'But this place takes a lot of upkeep. We thought it best to ask now if you'd prefer us to sell up and buy something smaller. The alternative is to carry on as we are and trust that at least one of you will be in a position to keep the place on when the time comes.'

Leonie felt winded. In Italy it had been a constant source of comfort to know that Friars Wood was there to run home to whenever she wanted.

'The thing is, Dad,' said Adam, looking suddenly older than his twenty-one years, 'I won't be in a position to take it on for a long time yet. And unless Leonie and Jess marry millionaires or win the lottery they won't be able to either, not to mention Kate and Fenny.'

Tom Dysart filled his pipe with deliberation, then outlined the plan he had in mind to provide security for his family and the home they all loved so much. The sensible course, he told them, was the one his father had taken. The property had been arranged so that it had remained in the possession of the senior Dysarts until one of them died, afterwards to pass jointly into the hands of the surviving parent and Tom, who had been designated heir to the house. 'Originally your mother and I restored and redecorated the Stables, meaning to live in it ourselves, but when it was ready your grandparents liked the result so much they persuaded us to let them live there instead, and left the care of the house to us. After both parents died I was to provide Rachel with a sum of money to the value of half the property.

Fortunately they both lived to a good age, so I was in a position to do that fairly comfortably when the time came, however much Rachel protested she didn't need it all.'

'Then can't you do that with Adam?' said Leonie quickly.

'I had only one sister,' her father pointed out.

Leonie shivered. 'I've always taken it for granted that Adam would inherit Friars Wood. Look, Dad, I'd willingly forgo my claim to any money as long as he's able to hang onto it.' She gave her brother a wry little smile. 'And lets us all come home to roost from time to time.'

'I feel the same,' said Jess fervently.

'I hate this,' said Kate in despair. 'I just want Friars Wood to stay in the family.'

'So say all of us,' said Adam, and looked at his father squarely. 'We'll do anything it takes to secure that, Dad.'

Leonie gave him a teasing smile. 'What happens if you fall for someone who doesn't fancy sharing with four sisters?'

'I'll send her packing,' said Adam promptly.

Everyone laughed, lightening the atmosphere slightly as Tom Dysart went on to explain that this arrangement would help with inheritance tax, but it also meant that when one parent died, whoever was left in joint ownership would be obliged to look after the survivor.

'Which is not as much of a problem as it might be because of the Stables,' said Frances briskly. 'Either one of us would be quite happy to move in there, even both of us together at some stage, just as my in-laws did.'

'Adam's the obvious choice to inherit,' said Leonie firmly. 'He's the only son, and he's also going to follow you into the auction house, Dad, so in the normal way of things he's the only one certain to remain in the area.'

Adam gave his parents a very sober, thoughtful look. 'You mean that some time in the future—hopefully a very long time in the future—if the property comes solely to me, the value of it, and any money you leave us, would all be divided into equal portions, and I'd hand the girls' shares over.'

Jess shook her head. 'Impossible with so many of us. No one could expect you to do that. It was different for Dad with only Rachel.'

'I couldn't do it right now,' Adam agreed, a stubborn jut to his chin, 'but when the time comes I'll make damn sure I can.'

'Or,' said his father, 'I could accept the offer and buy a smaller place, and have a lot more money in the bank afterwards.'

Four pairs of eyes gazed at him in horror.

'You don't mean that, do you, Dad?' demanded Leonie.

'I'm just mentioning it as an option. An option which isn't open for long,' he added. 'I've been given a week or two to consider it before it's withdrawn.'

'I'd rather you didn't consider it at all,' said Adam, his young face stern below the mop of curly black hair. 'I've got Finals coming up. I'd rather not have this hanging over me when I go back. Couldn't we settle it now?'

'I'm all for that,' said Jess quickly. 'If this is a democratic meeting, are we allowed to vote?'

Tom smiled wryly. 'Of course you are. Hands up all those in favour of staying, and letting Adam take over Friars Wood one day, along with all its responsibilities.'

Five hands shot up, and Tom grinned at his wife and followed suit.

'Unanimous,' said Leonie with satisfaction, and gave

her brother a reassuring smile. 'Don't worry, Adam. When the time comes we won't dun you for the money.'

'Amen to that,' said Jess, slumping in her chair. 'You can have my share, Adam, as long as you hang onto Friars Wood.'

'Mine too,' said Kate thankfully.

'Thank you, ladies, but if I can possibly manage it no sacrifices will be required. Who knows? Perhaps I'll discover a hidden Rembrandt one day and sell it for millions,' declared Adam, jumping up with some of his usual energy restored. 'Time I was off. By the way, Dad,' he added, 'who made the offer?'

'A London company,' said his mother, getting to her feet. 'Now then, Adam, get a move on, or you'll be late back.'

After Adam had been waved on his way, Leonie suggested her father took Fenny for a walk with the dog, and sent her mother off for a rest while she and Kate saw to the clearing up. The still-suffering Jess was ordered to sit down and save herself for the drive back to London later, an instruction she complied with gratefully.

'Thanks, you two. I don't mind telling you I'm a bit bushed,' she admitted. 'A busy week followed by last night's party, with Dad's bombshell on top of it—' She blew out her cheeks. 'I'm in a state of shock.' She heaved herself out of her chair. 'But this won't do. I'd better get my stuff together so I'm ready for the off when Mother gets up.'

Jess's loud cry of indignation a minute later sent Kate and Leonie running upstairs to ask what the matter was.

'Mother isn't resting; she's tidying our rooms,' Jess said wrathfully.

Frances smiled unrepentantly. 'I'm just changing the

beds. Mrs Briggs will do the bedrooms properly in the morning.' She gave Jess a stern look. 'And mind you get an early night when you get back, Jessamy Dysart. You've got dark rings under your eyes.'

'Yes, Mother,' said her daughter meekly, flushing slightly as she intercepted a sparkling glance from Leonie. 'In bed by ten, I promise.'

In the evening, when Kate was finishing off homework in her room, and Fenny was fast asleep in bed after the exertions of the night before, Leonie settled down on a sofa in the study with the dog snoring gently on the rug beside her. Not quite ready to collapse in a heap, as she'd told Chris Morgan, she was tired enough to put her feet up as she looked through the Sunday papers while her parents watched a serial they were following on television.

Pitying her siblings on their respective motorway journeys, Leonie relaxed, feeling deeply glad of her unexpected break at home. Adam rang at one stage to say he'd arrived safely, and eventually Jess reported in with the same message.

'She said the traffic was awful, it rained most of the way, and she was going to bed the minute she'd eaten something,' reported Frances, returning.

Kate came down to say she was going to bed, and a little later Leonie volunteered to make tea. As she returned with a loaded tray she paused in the hall to relocate the wobbling teapot, then stiffened as she realised her parents were talking over the lunchtime discussion. She stood rooted to the spot for a moment as she listened, then retreated silently along the hall. After a pause she went back towards the study, rattling the tray a little to herald her arrival. She poured tea for her mother, handed her father a whisky, then announced that she fancied some air.

'I'll take Marzi for a stroll,' she announced casually. 'After that I think I'll get myself to bed.' She clicked her fingers to the dog, then went to collect a coat and rubber boots.

After a forage round the garden as far as the Eyrie and back, Leonie left the dog with her parents and said goodnight. But instead of going to bed she consulted a telephone directory, put her cellphone in a pocket, then stole out again into the night and crossed the courtyard to the Stables. Using her torch to do some brief, surreptitious telephoning, she put the phone back in her pocket, then shone a light on the long-unused, overgrown path which led from Adam's back door along the edge of the cliff. It was hard going, and dangerously slippery with mud in places, with untamed bushes and snares of brambles that tore at her jacket, but the adrenaline from her anger sent Leonie storming along the route she'd used so often in her childhood.

After a while heavy rain began to fall, and moonlight gave way to streaming darkness, but she slithered on, glad when the path took a familiar turn at last to lead inland to an old gate hidden in the encroaching undergrowth. When she wrestled the rusty catch open the gate crashed into the bushes, resisting all her efforts to get it back in place behind her, and in the end Leonie abandoned it impatiently and continued her struggle through a belt of woodland far more densely tangled than she remembered. She emerged, dishevelled and panting at last, into what had once been one of the most beautiful gardens in the area. As she gained easier going through a dilapidated walled garden, a squall blew up from the Wye and the rain came down in torrents, drenching her.

The dark, looming shape of the house looked unfamiliar and oddly menacing by the meagre light of her torch beam, and Leonie hurriedly turned her back on it to make for the welcoming lights of a small lodge near the closed iron gates. Sodden and breathless, she hammered furiously on the lodge door, which flew open almost at once. And Jonah Savage stood there, his face blank with astonishment as he identified his visitor.

'*Leo?* What's wrong? Has something happened? Come in, you're soaked to the skin. Don't tell me you came here on foot!'

Leonie stood just inside the door, careless of the muddy water she was dripping everywhere. 'I've just learned that you've made my father an offer for Friars Wood,' she spat, and thrust strands of wet hair away from her accusing eyes. 'Wasn't it enough to ruin my life all those years ago? Now you want to take my home away from me as well!'

CHAPTER FOUR

JONAH stood in silence, like a man turned to stone. 'I think you've got that slightly wrong, Leonie,' he drawled at last.

'You mean you haven't made an offer for my home?' she demanded.

'No. I made the offer right enough. I was referring to your other accusation, my dear Miss Dysart. It was you who ruined *my* life—for a while, at least,' he added, with deliberate insult.

'How dare you say that?' Her voice shook with feelings she'd kept suppressed so long they threatened to overwhelm her now she'd slackened her guard. 'You were the unfaithful one, not me.'

'Unfaithful?' His eyes narrowed dangerously. 'What the devil are you talking about? I never looked at another woman from the moment I met you.'

'That's not true,' she threw back at him, feeling sick at the very thought of it.

Jonah thrust her aside without ceremony, and locked the door. 'I refuse to discuss this here. You'd better come to the kitchen first and get that wet coat off. Do your parents know where you are?'

'No. They think I'm in bed,' she admitted.

Jonah threw her a flaying look. 'And what happens when they find you are not?' He seized the telephone, stabbed in the numbers for Friars Wood, and when Tom Dysart answered Jonah gave him Leonie's whereabouts, telling him he'd run her back when she'd dried off.

'How did you know I'd be here?' he demanded. 'For all you knew I might have been on my way back to Pennington, or even London.'

'I rang just now to make sure.'

'So that was you,' he said grimly. 'Take your boots off. And the socks.' He led the way into the cramped, old-fashioned kitchen, where a stained old Aga gave out welcome warmth. He draped the socks over the front rail, held out his hand for her coat, and shook it, then gave her a towel and told her to dry her hair. She rubbed at the damp, tightly curling mass, her adrenaline slowly replaced by a strong suspicion that she'd been a fool to charge over here in a temper. Now it was too late she could see, with depressing clarity, that she should have slept on her anger and confronted Jonah in the morning, in cold blood.

'You're shivering,' he observed without sympathy. 'I'm afraid this place is only barely habitable, but there's a fire in the other room. Go and sit by it. I'll make some coffee.'

In the little sitting room the brand-new sofa and workmanlike desk and office chair were very different from the chintz and comfortable clutter of Mrs Baxter, wife of the Brockhill head gardener in the past. A laptop lay open on the desk beside a pile of ancient-looking deeds Jonah had obviously been working on before the interruption. Heartily sorry, now, for the furious impulse which had propelled her here, Leonie sat on the edge of the sofa and stretched out cold bare feet to the warmth of flames crackling round stacked logs in the fireplace.

When Jonah came in she tucked her feet back quickly, and received a mug of coffee with brief thanks, mortified because her teeth were chattering too much to let her drink.

'Are you that cold?' he demanded. 'Or do you feel ill?'

She shook her head. 'It's reaction. I lost my temper—something I try to avoid,' she added bitterly. 'The only one who ever suffers by it is me.'

'I disagree with that,' he retorted, and sat down in the desk chair. 'You were very obviously in a rage when you wrote that famous letter.'

Leonie waited for the shivering to subside. 'Actually I wasn't,' she said, when she could speak distinctly. 'I'm not sure what the word is for the way I felt. Disillusion, shock, and as if the bottom had suddenly dropped out of my world. Is there one word to describe all that?'

'If there isn't there should be,' he said bitingly. 'It just about sums up my own reaction when you sent my ring back.'

Leonie raised a doubting eyebrow and stared into the fire. 'If you say so.'

'You really believe you were the only one who suffered?' he demanded.

'No,' she admitted reluctantly. 'I think you did care for me once—'

'*Care* for you?' Jonah sprang up and stalked towards her, to turn her face up to his with an ungentle hand, his eyes as sharp and cold as icicles as they bored into hers. 'At the risk of sounding melodramatic, Miss Dysart, your letter was a stab to the heart.'

She pushed his hand away. 'It was meant to be,' she said malevolently, and succeeded in drinking some of the coffee.

Jonah sat down on the fender, arms folded. 'So, Leonie, I didn't ask you to come here tonight, but now you are here you can damn well give me an explanation at last.'

'Oh, please,' she said wearily. 'Why keep up the act?'

He leaned forward to emphasise his words. 'Because I'm not guilty, Leo. You condemned me for a crime I didn't commit. From the moment I first saw you there was never anyone else. And,' he added with menace, 'whoever told you so was a malicious liar.'

She swallowed sickly, regretting the coffee. 'No one told me. I found out all by myself.'

He frowned. 'Found what out?'

Leonie suddenly lost patience. 'We could go on and on like this all night, so I vote we drop the subject and revert to the little matter of Friars Wood.' Her eyes glittered darkly as they met his. 'Tell me, Jonah, did you make my father the offer for it out of revenge?'

Jonah gave her a patronising smile. 'My dear girl, you flatter yourself. It was a simple matter of business. My company recently acquired Brockhill, to develop the property and turn it into luxury apartments. After consultation with the board I made your father an offer which would have allowed me to do the same with Friars Wood, which stands on land that was once part of the Brockhill property.' He paused, his eyes narrowing to a gleam which turned her cold. 'I gave Tom time to think the offer over, of course, but this evening I've made a discovery. Before you came hammering on my door so dramatically I was looking through the deeds. I turned up something very interesting.'

Something about his attitude made Leonie's heart pound. 'What was it?'

Jonah smiled lazily. 'As I said, Friars Wood stands on land once purchased from the Laceys of Brockhill.'

'I know that. My great-grandfather bought it from his friend. Theodore Lacey owned most of the land round here at the time.'

'How fascinating,' said Jonah mockingly. 'Unfortunately, the document in question shows that some mistake was made about the extent of the sale. To cut through the legal jargon, half an acre of your father's property—the part where the Stables now stands, plus the strip which runs right down the road and allows access to Friars Wood, legally belongs to JS Developments.'

Leonie felt the blood drain from her face. 'So what does this mean?' she asked at last. 'Are you saying that if my father doesn't want to sell he's forced to pay you for the land he thought he owned all along?'

'More or less,' agreed Jonah affably.

'What sort of money are we talking about?'

The sum Jonah mentioned took Leonie's breath away. 'Of course,' he said, eyeing her, 'there are ways of getting round this particular problem if Tom doesn't wish to sell.'

'Ways?' she repeated, incensed by his casual use of her father's name. 'What are you implying? My father would never countenance anything remotely irregular.'

'I'm well aware of that.' Jonah paused deliberately. 'But because you love Friars Wood so much maybe *you* could, Leonie.'

Her eyes flashed ominously. 'What do you mean? I don't possess that kind of money.'

'I wasn't thinking of money.'

His smile sent the blood rushing back into Leonie's face. 'I don't understand,' she said tightly.

Jonah shook his head in mock reproof. 'Oh, come now. I think you understand very well.'

'Are you suggesting I—I *sell* myself in exchange for a plot of land?' Leonie's mouth twisted in distaste. 'Get real, Jonah. You may be some kind of squire now, but I'm no village—' She stopped short, cursing herself as Jonah smiled.

'Maiden? I know, Leo, I know,' he agreed, eyes glittering. 'I was your first lover, remember?'

She remembered all too vividly, even after seven long years of doing her utmost to forget.

'It's very good of you to offer, of course,' he continued kindly, getting to his feet. 'But I was thinking of a different kind of trade, one which doesn't involve your physical charms. Much as I still appreciate them. You were attractive enough before, but with a touch of maturity you're almost beautiful.'

Leonie suddenly lost it completely. She jumped up and slapped his face with a force that snapped his head back. 'Do what you like with your poxy land,' she threw at him, then gasped as Jonah's hands clamped on her upper arms, the handprint on his face deepening in colour as the ice in his eyes gave way to a fury she'd never seen in them before.

'Don't, Jonah,' she said in hoarse entreaty, struggling to free herself.

'You knew the risk you were running when you came here tonight,' he rasped, and pulled her into a crushing embrace she knew, from experience, she had no hope of escaping until he released her. But in the past she'd always yielded to it gladly, lovingly, exulting in her power to arouse him. A power it was alarmingly obvious she still possessed. He pulled her closer, thrusting his knee between her thighs, his eyes blazing into hers as one hand clamped her wrists together behind her back, the other thrusting beneath her sweater to caress her breasts, which hardened in traitorous response. Leonie uttered a choked protest and fought like a tigress, willing herself to show no response, but Jonah's relentless, knowing fingers teased and stroked, rolling erect nipples between thumb and forefinger to send fiery sensation streaking down to the part of her which throbbed in traitorous, moist response. Jonah's mouth closed over hers, stifling her protests, his conquering lips and tongue reducing her to gasping, pulsating silence as he pushed her back down on the sofa, and as the final insult took the last of her breath away by lying full length on top of her. She glared up into his taut, implacable face, her chest heaving as he met the blaze in her eyes with a smile of triumph. She turned her face away, striving for cold indifference, then gasped in outrage as he unzipped her jeans, his seeking fingers probing between her thighs. She reared up in renewed, frenzied protest, but with merciless expertise he brought her to a solitary, gasping climax she could neither prevent nor disguise. Hot with shame, angry tears leaking from her closed eyes, she fought to control the breath tearing through her lungs, bracing herself for what she was certain would come next. But instead of taking possession of her, as she'd expected, Jonah stood up and returned to the fire, leaning a hand on the chimneypiece as he gazed down into the dying fire.

'Put yourself back together,' he said harshly, without looking at her. 'I'll drive you home.'

Leonie scrambled to her feet, pushing tangled hair out of her eyes, shuddering with humiliation and rage as she knuckled the tears away. She yanked her sweater down and zipped up her jeans with shaking, clumsy fingers. 'Right,' she spat at his back. 'I suppose I invited all that by coming here tonight. I was a fool, but at least now we're quits. You've had your retaliation at last. I hope you're satisfied—'

'Satisfied? Wrong word, Leo.' Jonah turned round, and Leonie's face flamed as she realised why he'd kept his back to her. His jeans were old, and fitted so closely there was no mistaking his arousal.

'My aim,' said Jonah very deliberately, 'was to prove a point. Which I did, very conclusively. I wouldn't have sought you out to make the experiment, but you took it on yourself to come here of your own free will. So when you let fly at me I couldn't resist the temptation.'

'Yet you did resist it, ultimately.' Her voice shook with illogical rage at the thought of it.

He eyed her with polite interest. 'Were you certain I meant to have you?'

'I assumed you were going to carry on to the logical conclusion, yes.' Her eyes narrowed suddenly. 'So what were you doing, Jonah? Proving that my flesh was weaker than yours? That you had the self-control to abstain?' She dropped her eyes to the tell-tale proof of his desire. 'Or are you saving yourself for someone else? If so, I'm impressed. Fidelity, as I know only too well, isn't your strongest point.'

'Have you finished?' Jonah's voice was so deadly quiet Leonie took an involuntary step back. 'Don't worry,' he assured her. 'I shan't touch you again. So sit down. And listen.'

'I thought you were ready to drive me back,' she began, but the look in his eyes silenced her. Burning with resentment, she resumed her place on the sofa, refusing to look at him.

'Before you go let's return to the trade we were discussing before your temper got the better of you,' he observed dispassionately. 'And a word of advice—be careful who you assault in future, Leonie. Another time you might not get off so lightly.'

Lightly! 'Don't worry,' she said bitterly. 'I've never hit anyone before, nor am I likely to again.'

He nodded approvingly. 'Good. Your Latin lover, for instance, might not be so forbearing.'

Leonie controlled herself with effort. 'It's getting late,' she said tightly, 'so just tell me what you want in exchange for the land and I'll go home—whether you drive me or not. I can always go back the way I came.'

'Don't be childish, Leo. Of course I'll drive you,' he said impatiently. 'Very well. My requirements are simple. I'll make the land over to your father if you give me a full explanation, here and now, as to why you left me.'

Leonie stared at him blankly. 'You can't be serious! You're prepared to barter a valuable plot of land just to hear me tell you something you already know?'

'For God's sake,' he said with sudden violence, 'I *don't* know. That's the point.' He leaned forward, his eyes locked with hers. 'I won't pretend that I've never looked at another woman since you *left* me. But I swear I was never unfaithful to you while we were together. I loved you, Leo. And, fool that I am, I thought you loved me.'

'I did,' she said passionately. 'You know I did.' Her eyes glistened suddenly with unshed tears. 'But one day I just happened to be in the wrong place at the wrong time. And my whole life fell apart.'

Jonah looked at her in expectant silence which stretched Leonie's nerves to the limit. Then a log crashed in the fireplace and broke the spell. He added more logs to the blaze, then sat down beside her, leaving a careful space between them.

Leonie sat very still, her eyes dry now as she stared at the flames curling up around the new logs. 'All right,

Jonah, I'll explain,' she said wearily, 'but I want your promise that you'll never mention this again. To me or anyone else.'

'You have it,' he assured her, and took her hand.

She was tempted to snatch it away, but in the end let it stay in his hard, familiar grasp. 'Before I start there's something I need to know. You're not the only one after the truth, Jonah.' She turned to look at him. 'How many people actually know that Fenny is your daughter?'

CHAPTER FIVE

JONAH stared at her in such outrage that for the first time Leonie felt the cold frisson of doubt.

'You actually believe I'm the father of Rachel's child?' He flung her hand away as though her touch contaminated him, his eyes lambent with distaste.

'I know you are,' she lashed out. 'I was there that day.'

'*What* day?' he snarled.

Leonie flinched, and Jonah clenched his teeth, controlling himself with obvious effort.

'I've no idea what you're talking about,' he said at last, 'so explain. Start from the beginning.'

Leonie had returned to Friars Wood for the Easter holiday, and spent the last weekend of it in London in Jonah's flat before flying back to Italy for the final term, then coming home to marry him. They had met at a party given by Rachel Dysart during the summer vacation the previous year, and long before Leonie was due to go back to Florence Jonah had proposed, and was rapturously accepted. After she left they exchanged long, passionate letters, and a small fortune was spent on phone calls until they were reunited at Christmas, which Jonah spent at Friars Wood with the Dysarts, afterwards taking Leonie to stay with his parents over New Year.

The Easter holiday was spent in much the same way, except for the final weekend alone together in his flat, talking over preparations for the wedding and bemoaning the coming separation. Jonah was unable to make the promised visit to Florence, because he was about to fly to New Zealand to represent JS Developments in a business deal in Auckland. They spent a shamelessly large proportion of their time in bed, their passion heightened by the looming separation, and it was a pale, hollow-eyed pair of lovers who parted early that foggy Monday morning, Jonah for his office, and Leonie to take a taxi to Heathrow.

'Don't come with me. Let's say goodbye here, in private,' she'd implored. 'I hate airport partings.'

'How about airport meetings?' he teased. 'You don't want me waiting when you come back?'

Leonie gave him her answer without words, and he responded in kind, kissing her with a mounting passion which made it hard for her to tear herself away when the taxi arrived. The fog was thicker than either she or Jonah had noticed in their absorption with each other, and she was late arriving at the terminal, to discover that her flight was cancelled, all other flights were delayed, and she had parted from Jonah hours before she need have done. A hurried, persuasive interlude with the airline staff resulted in the exchange of her ticket for a flight next day, and a phone call to Florence to inform the school of the delay.

In her jubilation Leonie's next thought was to ring Jonah and tell him the glad news, then her eyes lit with sudden anticipation. Much better to return to the flat and surprise him when he got home. She made the return journey by underground, and by the time she arrived back she was feeling the effects of her sleep-starved weekend so much the prospect of a nap in Jonah's bed was irresistible.

Leonie woke with a start later that fateful Monday afternoon, to the sound of voices in the other room. She sat up in dismay, not at all pleased to find that Jonah had company. Then her eyes widened as she identified Jonah's visitor. The bedroom door was slightly ajar, allowing the desolation in the woman's voice to come through very clearly, and Leonie's first instinct was to run from the room to offer comfort. Then the import of what she was hearing struck her like a physical blow.

'Are you sure?' demanded Jonah urgently.

'Sure?' said Rachel Dysart, and gave an embittered little laugh. 'Oh, yes, Jonah. I'm sure. And after fainting in your father's office an hour ago I imagine everyone else will be sure before long. You were sweet to rescue me.'

'It seemed best to haul you out of there. Dad was in a terrible state.'

'Not the behaviour he expects from his personal assistant!'

'He was worried about you, Rachel. So was I,' Jonah added emphatically.

'Sorry I had to stop to be sick on the way. Horribly embarrassing.'

'Not to me. It seemed best to bring you here for a bit as it's nearer.'

'Good move. But I'd like to go home now.'

To Leonie's horror she heard Jonah suggesting a short rest on his bed first, but to her overwhelming relief this was vetoed.

'No, thanks,' said Rachel, her voice suddenly unsteady. 'Look, Jonah, I meant what I said in the car. I'm sorry to burden you like this, but now you know you must see that the situation's impossible. Under the circumstances I really must resign. Frankly, I don't know how I've carried on so long. So in the morning I'll give your father my notice.'

There was a rustle, and Leonie felt suddenly sick as she realised Jonah had taken Rachel in his arms. 'I understand,' she heard him say, with a note of tenderness which cut her to the heart. 'But will you be all right? You know I'll do everything in my power to help.'

'Then persuade your father to let me go as soon as possible,' said Rachel thickly. 'I'll be forty-one in a week's time, a bit past it for first-time motherhood. I'm exhausted. And it's getting to be an uphill struggle to disguise the fact that I'm more than six months pregnant.'

'Six *months*!' Jonah swore softly. 'Why the hell didn't you tell me before?'

'I haven't told anyone.' There was a pause. 'I'll have to let Tom and Frances know, of course. But otherwise, Jonah,' added Rachel, in a commanding voice, 'no one must ever know the truth.'

'That's impossible—' said Jonah fiercely.

'No,' was the peremptory interruption. 'You know perfectly well why. She must never know. Swear you won't tell her, Jonah. It would break her heart. You know it would. I can cope with everything else. But not that.'

The moment she was sure they'd gone Leonie got up to dress, blinded by tears, trembling so much she was all fingers and thumbs. She rang for a taxi, then took her luggage back downstairs to the hall to wait, and when the cab arrived told the driver to take her to a hotel near Heathrow. She sat like a statue on the journey, checked in at the hotel, then lay limp as a rag doll on the bed, blind to her surroundings as she came to terms with her discovery.

Rachel, the much-loved aunt she'd always looked up to with such enormous admiration, was expecting Jonah

Savage's child. The child of the man Rachel's niece had been due to marry. Leonie let out a cry of sharp, physical pain and turned on her face.

Rachel Dysart was a handsome woman, tall and fair, like her brother Tom, with a lithe figure women years her junior envied, her body shape lending itself to pregnancy without revealing the fact too early. Leonie shuddered, remembering how she'd teased Rachel about putting on weight, how Rachel's usual power-dressing had given way to softer clothes that draped and concealed. She'd even accused her aunt of having a secret lover...

Leonie bolted suddenly for the bathroom and surrendered to violent retching which went on and on until she was shivering uncontrollably, her misery so intense she would have traded her soul to run home to Friars Wood and hurl herself into her mother's arms. But that was impossible. Because Rachel was involved. Leonie gritted her teeth. She would just have to bear her pain alone and go back to Florence. When she was there, and she felt a bit calmer, she'd write to Jonah and tell him everything was over between them. The letter would be waiting for him when he got home from New Zealand. The delay would be all to the good. By then she'd be hardened to the idea of him as ex-lover. She'd get rid of the cellphone he'd given her, and if he rang the school she'd leave instructions that she was unavailable. Her only hope of recovery would be never to see or speak to him again. And she would volunteer to work at the school's summer camp in Umbria to keep out of Rachel's way when the baby was born. *Jonah's* baby. At the prospect Leonie's renewed storm of weeping was so prolonged that her eyes were still swollen when she arrived in Florence, and she had to lie about a cold.

*   *   *

Jonah heard Leonie out in complete silence punctuated only by a furious gesture of denial at certain points in her story. When she'd finished he got up without a word and went from the room. She stared after him, biting her lip, wondering what to do, but to her surprise he returned with a bottle of whisky and two glasses.

'I know you don't like it,' he said, forestalling her refusal. 'Unless your tastes have changed, of course,' he added curtly. 'But I think the situation calls for something a lot stronger than coffee.'

Jonah was furiously angry, Leonie realised with resentment. As though she were the one at fault.

He handed her a glass with an inch of whisky in it and told her to drink it down. Leonie obeyed, grimacing at the taste, but glad of the warmth as the spirit did its work. Jonah sipped his more sparingly, and sat, legs outstretched, on the battered leather fender, his face inscrutable.

'Quite a story,' he observed at last.

'But the gospel truth,' she snapped, infuriated by Jonah's lack of remorse.

'Only part of it.'

Leonie frowned. 'Are you denying that Fenny's your daughter?'

'Of course I deny it,' he said scornfully. 'When—or if—I have a child, you can be damned sure I won't leave it to someone else to bring up.'

Leonie gazed at him dumbly, shaken to the depths. She'd arrived fuelled by blazing certainty about Jonah's sins, yet his denial had the unmistakeable ring of truth. 'I don't believe you,' she said at last, more from habit than conviction.

'Would I lie about something like this?' he demanded.

Leonie stared at his taut, angry face. 'But she's the

image of you. The shiny black hair, those unmistakable eyes—'

'Kate's eyes are hazel, too,' he reminded her.

'Hers are more gold, not green like yours—and Fenny's.' She drew in a deep, ragged breath and held out her glass. 'Could I have some more?'

'No. I prefer to restore you to your parents in relatively sober condition.'

Leonie stood up. 'Then restore me right now, please.'

'Stay where you are,' he ordered. 'You don't get off that easily, Leo.'

'I know you're angry, Jonah—' she began, but his hand made a chopping motion, silencing her.

'Angry?' He gave a bark of derisive laughter. 'You just don't get it, do you? You took it on yourself to ruin two lives when a simple explanation would have put everything right between us in minutes. You bet I'm angry, Miss Dysart. And you're damn well going to sit there until you know the truth. Though it's too late to mend anything now. Things could never be the same between us again. Despite,' he added, with a look in his eyes which brought the blood rushing to her face, 'our continued rapport in the sex department. I won't deny that I still lust after you. But right now, Leonie, I don't like you very much.'

His words acted like salt on an open wound, but she lifted her chin proudly and motioned him to go on. 'Have your say, then, and I'll go.'

'Sit down,' he ordered.

Leonie resumed her place on the sofa, partly because she felt at a disadvantage with bare feet, but mainly because she was filled with sudden dread. If Jonah wasn't the father of Rachel's child, who was?

Jonah took some time to begin. He stared down into

his glass, as though looking into a crystal ball which revealed the past. 'I admit I was very fond of Rachel,' he began at last. 'But I didn't look on her as a contemporary. She was my father's right hand, and knew far more about the business than I did when I joined the firm. I'd worked on various building sites during university vacations and so on, but when it came to management I was still wet behind the ears.'

Rachel Dysart, personal assistant to James Savage, the founder of JS Developments, had been a great help to Jonah from day one as he'd begun to work his way up through the company. Often she'd acted as buffer between her boss and the heir apparent, when their formidable temperaments had clashed, and it had been Rachel who'd trained up an efficient secretary for Jonah when he'd reached the status which required one.

'Then one day Rachel invited a few JS people to a drinks party at her flat and included me. And you surprised her by turning up out of the blue.' Jonah eyed her quizzically. 'I assume you remember the occasion?'

'Oh, yes,' Leonie said dully. 'One way and another, how could I forget?'

'She'd never asked me to her place before—because I was the boss's son, I suppose. And unless you were staying with her,' he added with emphasis, 'I was never there again. The only other place I ever met Rachel, apart from the office, was at Friars Wood once you and I were engaged.'

'But the day I went back to your flat—'

'Rachel had shocked everyone by passing out while she was taking the minutes of a meeting.' Jonah smiled grimly. 'All the suits were in a right old panic, including my father, so I picked her up and carried her into my office. Father wanted to send for a doctor, but Rachel came round quickly and asked to leave to see her own. I volunteered to drive her, but she was so ill in the car I took her to my place until she felt fit enough to make it to hers.'

'I know,' said Leonie despondently. 'I heard you talking.'

'Unfortunately you didn't hear everything,' he retorted. The bright, cold eyes locked with hers. 'And of course you know what happened after that.'

Leonie nodded, her eyes bright with unshed tears. Rachel had been coming down with flu when Jonah had taken her home to his flat. By the time Leonie had been back in Florence, and Jonah in New Zealand, Rachel's flu had turned to pneumonia, which had precipitated the premature birth of her daughter. She had survived only long enough to receive Frances and Tom's promise to bring her baby up as their own. Grief-stricken, Leonie had begged two days' leave but had flown back to Florence immediately after the funeral, missing Jonah by hours.

'I'll always be sorry I couldn't make it,' he said sombrely. 'My parents were at the funeral, of course, but they drove to Heathrow afterwards to pick me up and took me home with them. The phone I gave you never answered, and the staff at your school, after I finally managed to get through to them, informed me you'd moved to a different apartment in Florence. So I rushed round to my place, sure I'd find a letter from you. And sure enough, I did, but with your engagement ring in it instead of your new address. The rest, as they say, is history.'

Leonie waited after he'd finished speaking, finding it hard to break the lengthening silence to ask the question Jonah had left unanswered. Eventually he roused himself from his reverie and turned to look at her. 'Didn't you wonder, sometimes, why an attractive woman like Rachel never married?'

'Of course—we all did. Dad used to tease her about it all the time. But Rachel always laughed it off, saying she was married to her career.' Leonie's mouth twisted. 'But that was obviously a front.'

'Do you believe me, Leo?' he asked abruptly.

She gave him a long, introspective look. 'Yes, I think I do.'

'Why?'

She shrugged. 'It sounds like the truth, I suppose.'

'Something I could have told you years ago, given the chance,' he said harshly. 'Lord knows I tried hard enough to see you, talk to you, ask what went wrong. Your family were very kind to me, but obviously just as much in the dark as I was. And in the end even the most persistent of lovers loses heart. *And* interest.'

She flinched. 'Yes. I can see that. Though under the circumstances I can be forgiven for making a mistake—'

'Not by me,' he said bitterly.

This news was oddly cheering to Leonie. If Jonah felt as strongly as that he must still care for her a little. She blinked hard, unaware until that moment that she still wanted him to care for her.

'What's the matter?' he asked.

Leonie pulled herself together. 'The thing is, Jonah, I'm only human. I need to know the truth about Fenny, who her father actually is. Not that it matters from a Dysart point of view. We all think of her as ours, anyway. Another little sister. But with those eyes—' She stopped dead, staring at him in horror as she remembered someone else with eyes like Jonah's.

He shook his head, reading her like a book. 'Wrong again, Leo. Like me, my father's not the unfaithful kind.' He smiled crookedly. 'Fenny's neither my daughter, nor my little sister; she's *my* cousin, too.'

CHAPTER SIX

'You only met my uncle once,' said Jonah, as Leonie's eyes filled with dawning comprehension. 'At the party my parents gave to celebrate our engagement.'

Leonie remembered the beautiful summer day at the Hampstead house only too well. Flora Savage had decided on a garden party, with strawberries and champagne consumed at small tables shaded from the sun by large umbrellas, and for Leonie bliss had pervaded the entire occasion, making it too painful to look back on afterwards. Among the host of people introduced to her that day Leonie remembered Richard Savage for a very good reason. Tall, dark and elegant in a pale linen suit and sunglasses, he'd arrived pushing his wife Helen in the wheelchair she'd been confined to for years.

'Fenny is Richard's child,' said Jonah. 'But don't judge him—or Rachel—too severely. He was devoted to Helen, but the physical side of their marriage ended after the brain haemorrhage disabled her. And Richard was a lot younger than my father. He was a man in the prime of life.'

Leonie nodded sadly. 'He was a barrister, wasn't he? So how did Rachel meet him?'

'Dad just happened to invite him to one of the company functions Rachel used to organise so brilliantly. Helen couldn't always cope with that kind of thing, so on this particular occasion Richard went alone.'

Leonie looked at him sombrely. 'And he and Rachel had an affair.'

Jonah shook his head. 'No, Leo. They fell madly in love. As people do. But my parents never knew. Nor did I until Rachel told me.'

'Why did she tell you?'

He smiled wryly. 'Because when I found out she was pregnant I jumped to the same conclusion as you. For a hideous split-second I thought my father might be to blame. Rachel was seriously unamused. She gave me such a tongue-lashing that day in the car we had to stop for her to throw up. In the end she was forced to tell me about Richard, if only to scotch any doubts about my father. And on the strict understanding that I never told another soul. By then, of course, Richard had been dead for a couple of months, and Rachel made me swear that Helen would never find out the truth.'

'So that's who she meant. I thought it was me,' said Leonie sadly. 'Poor Helen. And poor Rachel, too.'

'Richard never even knew she was pregnant. When he was killed in that motorway pile-up she couldn't forgive herself for not telling him he'd fathered the child he'd longed for so much,' said Jonah sombrely.

Leonie felt her throat thicken. 'Mother told me Rachel had been under the weather for a while, but I was so—'

'So what?' he prompted.

She stared at him defiantly. 'So wrapped up in you I never noticed when I came home that Easter. Did *you* notice?'

'No, I didn't. And for exactly the same reason.' He shrugged. 'I liked and respected Rachel, but you were the sole focus of my attention. In those days, anyway.'

Leonie felt a stab of pain. 'Jonah, are you really the only one Rachel told?'

'I've no idea. I always wished I could tell them, but my parents can't possibly know, otherwise they would have wanted to see Fenny from the start. I can't answer for yours, of course.'

Their eyes met. 'They *must* know,' said Leonie, with sudden conviction. 'When they promised Rachel to bring up her baby she's bound to have told them before— before she died.'

'How did they explain Fenny to the rest of you?'

'They didn't, really—just said Rachel was no keener on marriage than she'd ever been, but had decided to have a baby and bring it up on her own. When she died she trusted her daughter to us, to love as our own little sister. Which was the absolute truth, as far as it went. The others were too grief-stricken about Rachel to do anything but accept it without questions. I, of course,' added Leonie bitterly, 'thought I knew better—or worse.'

'Did it ever colour your feelings towards Fenny?'

'Oddly enough, no.' She smiled wryly. 'One look and I was besotted from the first.'

He nodded. 'I can understand that. My acquaintance is more recent, but the same thing applies.'

Leonie stared into the fire. 'It's strange, isn't it? That Rachel died and poor fragile Helen survived the tragedy. How is she these days?'

'Surprisingly well. She wouldn't leave the house she'd shared with Richard, because he'd had it fitted up in every way possible for her to lead a normal life in it. But these days she lives on the ground floor, and her two widowed sisters share the rest of the house.' Jonah smiled a little. 'Helen says it's like a Chekhov play without the angst. She's taken up painting. And of course my parents see a lot of her.'

Leonie glanced at her watch and gasped in horror. 'Look at the time. I must go.'

'Right.' Jonah kicked the logs down in the fireplace. 'Your jacket must be dry by now.'

On the short journey to Friars Wood neither of them said very much. When the car drew up in front of the house their eyes met fleetingly.

'Will you come in?' asked Leonie.

'No, thanks. I've still got some work to do. Oh, by the way.' Jonah reached into his pocket and took out a rolled document. 'We made a bargain, so this is yours.'

Leonie eyed him with hauteur. 'I can't possibly take that from you, Jonah. If we owe you money we'll pay it.'

'Consider the debt paid,' he said flatly, and got out of the car to let her out. 'I dislike loose ends.'

Which put her firmly in her place. If Jonah had wanted revenge those four cruel little words had exacted it in full measure, if he only knew it. And, knowing Jonah, she thought bitterly, he probably knew it very well.

As they got out the pouring rain drenched them both, then the front door opened and Jonah dived back in the car. 'Goodnight. Make my apologies to your parents for bringing you home so late.' He closed the window, then reversed back along the terrace and out of sight.

Leonie thrust the document in her pocket, feeling suddenly so miserable she hated the thought of the questions awaiting her. But after one look at her face her mother said nothing by way of reproof when she let her in. 'For heaven's sake get in a hot bath and dry that hair, Leo. No doubt you had your reasons for chasing up there, but whatever they are they'll keep until morning. Or indefinitely, if you prefer it that way.'

In other words no one was going to demand explanations Leonie was reluctant to give.

'Sorry to keep you up, Mother,' she said penitently.

'Want some tea?'

'No, thanks.' Leonie managed a smile, then kissed her mother goodnight. 'All I want is a bath and bed.'

Leonie had hoped to fall into oblivion the moment her head touched the pillow, but the revelations of the night kept her tossing and turning most of the night. It was light before she slept, and when she woke the morning was half over. She rushed through a shower, pulled on jeans and sweater and ran downstairs to a boisterous welcome from Marzi. Mrs Briggs got up from the table immediately, dusters and polish at the ready.

'At last, darling,' said Frances, smiling. 'We've been drinking coffee until you surfaced.'

'As long as you had a good rest, dear,' said Mrs Briggs placidly. 'All that flying about must be very tiring.'

'Not only the flying about, Mother,' said Leonie wryly, when they were alone. 'Sorry to be so late, though. I didn't even hear Fenny and Kate get up.'

'I managed to restrain Fenny, because you were sleeping so soundly it seemed a shame to disturb you.' Frances poured coffee. 'Want something to eat?'

'Not for the moment; I'll wait for lunch.' Leonie met her mother's eyes with remorse. 'Sorry about last night. Quite by accident I found myself eavesdropping on you and Dad, and heard that Jonah's company had made the offer for Friars Wood. So I charged up there to bawl him out.'

Frances rolled her eyes. 'I thought so! How did he take it?'

'He wasn't ecstatic to find me hammering on his door and throwing wild accusations at him, that's for sure.'

Leonie hesitated. 'Will Mrs Briggs be up there for a while?'

'An hour or so at the very least.' Frances Dysart smiled encouragingly. 'Something to get off your chest?'

'Last night Jonah told me who'd fathered Rachel's child,' said Leonie baldly. 'Did *you* know?'

Her mother blenched, then heaved in a deep, unsteady breath. 'Yes, darling, of course we did.'

'I thought you must have.' Leonie sighed despairingly. 'Why didn't you *tell* me?'

'But we couldn't, darling. Rachel swore us to secrecy about it, because Richard Savage's wife was still alive. But Jonah obviously knew. And if he's told you I suppose there's no point keeping it a secret any longer.' Frances shivered. 'Oh, Leo, that was the most horrible time. Soon after the shock of your break-up with Jonah I got an urgent call for help from Rachel. Imagine my reaction when I found she was not only pregnant but in the throes of pneumonia, which had brought on premature labour. I rang your father immediately, and he arrived at the hospital shortly before Fenny was born.' She got up and tore off a piece of kitchen paper to wipe her eyes. 'Thank God he was there in good time. At least Rachel died in the knowledge that Tom and I would bring her baby up and cherish her like our own. Which has been no hardship, heaven knows.'

'No. Fenny's easy to love,' agreed Leonie huskily. 'What did Rachel die of, exactly?'

'There were a lot of medical explanations. Apart from the pneumonia Rachel was undernourished and anaemic, from dieting to hide her pregnancy, and at an age when birth was more of a risk. Then when Richard died she worked harder than ever to combat her grief.' Frances sighed deeply. 'But in my opinion she simply died of a broken heart. Rachel was one of those rarities, a one-man woman. I believed Rachel when she told me Richard Savage loved her. But he loved his wife, too, and with Helen disabled divorce was never an option. Nor, Rachel assured me, did she want that. So when Richard died so suddenly I think the light just went out of Rachel's life.'

'You knew beforehand?'

'I knew Rachel had loved someone for years, but not who he was. When you and Jonah got engaged it was an added complication she hadn't bargained on, believe me.'

'So she wasn't matchmaking!' Leonie smiled a little.

'On the contrary. Rachel was always worried that Jonah would find out.'

'But she was forced to tell him the truth in the end.' Leonie described Jonah's rescue, when he'd taken Rachel home. Then took the plunge and described the misunderstanding responsible for the broken engagement.

Frances Dysart sat motionless for some time, obviously having trouble digesting this new revelation. 'I can't believe it!' she said at last. 'All these years you've thought Fenny was *Jonah's* daughter?'

'It may sound unbelievable to you, Mother, but if you'd been there in Jonah's flat that day you might have made the same mistake,' said Leonie defensively.

'No, I wouldn't, because I'd have marched out and confronted them,' said her mother roundly, and shook her head in wonder. 'Why did you never say anything? I could have put you right in seconds, my girl, deathbed promise or not.'

'How could I, Mother?' said Leonie passionately. 'Think about it! We all adored Rachel, Dad most of all.

After she was dead, no matter how much Fenny resembled Jonah, I couldn't spoil Rachel's memory for everyone.'

'No. I can understand that.' Frances sighed. 'Not that I see any resemblance to Jonah myself. I think Fenny looks like Kate. Lord, what a tangle. Anyway, it's out in the open now. I can even tell you that Adam won't have to pay anything to Fenny when he inherits. She was very generously provided for by Rachel, her entire education included.'

'Thank heavens for that!'

Frances paused, then gave her daughter a searching look. 'Leo, forgive me for prying, but if you and Jonah had all this out last night has it changed things between you?'

'You mean did he sweep me into his arms and tell me all was forgiven?' said Leonie flippantly. 'Afraid not, Mother. Jonah was violently angry. He made it very plain that it was too late to heal the rift.'

'I'm so sorry.' Frances looked at her searchingly. 'And how do you feel now you know the truth?'

'Depressed.' Leonie smiled forlornly. 'I made a complete mess of things, one way and another, didn't I? I'm only thankful Rachel never knew I broke with Jonah.' Her eyes widened in sudden dismay. 'You didn't tell her?'

'No, darling. By the time I reached Rachel there was no time to think of anything but the matter in hand. All my energy was given over to comfort and reassurance about her baby.' Her eyes filled with tears. 'I was very fond of her, you know.'

'It was mutual.' Leonie put out a hand to cover her mother's. 'Rachel once told me you were more to her than any sister could have been.'

'Did she really? How lovely.' Frances scrubbed at her eyes again and stood up. 'Come on. We can't let Mrs Briggs find us in floods of tears. Let's take Marzi for a walk while we have thoughts about dinner. Your father's got a busy day today. The contents of a minor stately home are going under the hammer.'

Dysart's was a respected auction house which had flourished in Pennington for three generations, and specialised in furniture, porcelain and silver, and some occasional fine art. Leonie's father was the current chairman, and employed a large, skilled staff, some of them left over from his father's day, and every one of them heart and soul in the business. Adam, to his father's infinite pleasure, had shown interest in the family concern since he was a small boy. These days he acted as porter in his vacations, revelling in the excitement when bidding grew frenzied over some sought-after item, and already skilled at nosing out bargains at the antiques fairs that were part of Dysart life.

That night Tom Dysart came home in celebratory mood after a successful day, and Fenny was allowed to stay up to hear about the sale before Leonie took her off to bed to read to her for a while.

Looking down from time to time at the shiny dark head against her shoulder, Leonie was assailed by so many emotions it was hard to keep her voice steady as she read. For years her belief about Jonah had kept her from seeing much of Fenny. Now she knew the truth she bitterly regretted the years of self-imposed exile. If she'd come right out with it and faced Jonah with her accusations at the very beginning they would have been married by now, with children of their own.

Fenny looked up, smiling, as Leonie came to the end

of the chapter. 'Will you read to me tomorrow night, too?'

'Every night until I go, darling.'

'I wish you didn't have to go at all,' said Fenny, snuggling down with her usual clutch of soft toys for company.

Leonie tucked her in, frowning thoughtfully as she realised she no longer had any reason to renew her contract with the school, unless she wanted to. Deferring thought about that until later, she kissed the upraised face lovingly. 'I'll stay longer next time,' she promised. 'Goodnight, sleep tight.'

Leonie left Fenny's door ajar to let in the landing light, then went along to Kate's room to find her sister at her desk, deep in revision. 'Don't you ever let up?' she asked, ruffling the wild dark curls.

'Not if I want good grades,' muttered Kate, then looked up with an absent smile. 'I'll take time off tomorrow night, Leo.'

'I'll bring you a hot drink later. Don't work too hard.'

When Leonie went downstairs she made a detour to the scullery to rummage in the pocket of the jacket she'd worn the night before, then joined her parents. 'By the way, Dad, just to complete your day of triumph, I've got something for you.' Smiling, she handed her father the yellowed document Jonah had given her.

Tom Dysart's eyebrows shot up as he studied the deed. 'How the devil did you come by this?'

'Mother's probably told you why I went barging over to Brockhill last night. Jonah gave me this before he brought me back,' said Leonie, flushing a little at the look her father gave her.

'We thought you were in bed,' he pointed out, looking over his glasses. 'If you feel the need for nocturnal ramblings in the future, Leonie, let us know first. It was hellish embarrassing to learn your whereabouts from Jonah.'

'Sorry, Dad,' she said in remorse. 'That was a one-off. It won't happen again.' She exchanged a glance with her mother. 'And on the plus side my visit to Brockhill cleared up a lot of misunderstandings last night.'

'So your mother tells me.' He shook his head. 'We could have cleared them up for you long since if we'd known. Though how you could imagine we'd have let Jonah in the house if you'd been right, I fail to see.' He turned back to the deed, studying it for a while, then grinned at her. 'Actually, I think Jonah was getting his own back, showing you this.'

'What do you mean?' demanded Leonie.

'A later document nullifies this one, darling. My father bought the extra bit of land when he took over Friars Wood.'

'Now, Leo, don't go flying off the handle again,' said Frances in alarm.

Leonie calmed herself with effort. 'Jonah told me the land was worth some vast sum,' she said tightly.

'But he gave it to you anyway?' Tom Dysart chuckled. 'Didn't he demand something in exchange?'

'Not my body, if that's what you're thinking,' she snapped, then bit her lip. 'Sorry, Dad. He just wanted my reasons for breaking our engagement.'

'An expensive bit of information at present-day valuation,' commented Frances.

'But does he know about the later transaction?' said Leonie, incensed to find she'd been conned.

'Of course he does.' Tom patted her hand. 'It's bound to be there in the records for Brockhill, same as ours for Friars Wood. I'm afraid you were had, Leo. Just be thankful it was only information Jonah wanted in return.'

CHAPTER SEVEN

KNOWING she deserved her father's teasing made it no easier to bear. Leonie sat with her parents for a while, then, too restless to sit still any longer, volunteered to make tea, and take some hot chocolate up for Kate. 'By the way, when Kate had the interview what did Trinity College ask by way of A-level grades?'

'Two Es,' said her father proudly.

'Wow! They must think she's a genius.' Leonie pulled a face. 'Good thing we'd got one academic in the family.'

'You got a very good degree yourself,' protested her mother.

'They demanded much higher grades from me at *my* hall of learning,' said Leonie wryly. 'Good thing Adam graduates this year. A bit of a strain on the finances to have them both in college together. Or will it be more expensive to pay Adam a wage at Dysart's?'

'Actually, no. A couple of people are retiring shortly. There'll be a shuffle up the ladder, and Adam will slot in at the bottom, just as I did in my day.' Tom smiled. 'And don't tell him I said so, but Adam's not only better at the business side of things, he's already got a better nose for a find than I had at his age. Answer that for me, darling,' he added as the phone rang.

When Leonie picked up the receiver in the hall she was flooded with guilt when she heard the husky tones of Roberto Forli, conscious that she'd hardly given him a thought during the hectic time at home. She assured him that all was well, and that she was missing him, and told him a little about the party. She was deliberately vague about the date of her return, and when he assured her that if she was away too long he would fly over to see her she agreed with enthusiasm, hoping Roberto couldn't tell it wasn't as warm as it might have been.

She didn't want Roberto to come. Not right now. Not with Jonah Savage in the vicinity. Besides, if Roberto were invited to visit her family he might read more into it than intended. She liked him very much. But, charming, sophisticated and attractive though he was, she didn't love him. Like Rachel, she thought bleakly, she was a one-man woman. Only the man didn't want her any more.

Leonie clenched her teeth as she remembered how easy Jonah had found it to con her. One mention of Friars Wood and the suspect land and she'd been up in arms, just as he'd intended. Not that he'd needed to resort to blackmail to hear the truth from her a last. From the moment they'd met on the train all the old pain and anger had come rushing back, and in the end she'd raced over to Brockhill to hurl her accusation of infidelity and revenge at him. But her volley had backfired, and left her squarely in the wrong. To be fair, she thought, staring out at the stars, he'd been entitled to his joke with the deed. And she had a depressing idea that if she expected him to ring her and ask to see her again she'd be disappointed. Just as she had been earlier, when she'd found her caller was Roberto Forli. Not Jonah Savage.

Next morning Leonie was up early, in time to meet her father on his way in from the morning ritual of throwing a ball for Marzi, and to share family breakfast before Tom dropped Kate and Fenny off at school on his way into Pennington. Leonie waved them off outside the Stables, promising to drive to pick the girls up in the afternoon, then decided a long walk would do her good. And benefit Marzi at the same time.

'Where's the dog, Mother?' she asked.

Frances emerged from the morning paper, looking about her vaguely. 'I've no idea. Tom always leaves him to make his own way back in the mornings. Wasn't he outside with you?'

Leonie shook her head and went out into the scullery, frowning when she found Marzi's bowl of food untouched. 'He hasn't had his breakfast,' she reported. 'I'd better look for him.'

She pulled on a jacket and ran out into the garden, frowning as she whistled and called. Marzi's appetite was at its height in the mornings, and he usually came running in from his first walk of the day to wolf down his meal. Leonie hurried along the cliff path to the Eyrie, the gazebo which gave a panoramic view of the Wye Valley. She hung as far as she dared over the pierced stone balustrade, peering down the steep drop to the river with growing concern, picturing the retriever injured and terrified after a fall down the cliff. When she was sure he wasn't visible anywhere she carried out a systematic search of the garden and checked every inch of the bluebell wood, which was a favourite haunt of Marzi's due to badgers, rabbits and the occasional fox scented there. Leonie shouted for him so much she was hoarse by the time she got back to the house.

'Has he come back?' she panted, bursting into the kitchen.

'No, he hasn't,' said her mother, alarmed. 'Where on earth can he have gone? Wait a minute—' She smiled in sudden relief. 'He had such a good time with the

Morgan dogs at the weekend he's probably taken off down to the farm.'

'Of course! Why didn't I think of that?' Leonie ran for the phone, but got Denzil Morgan's recorded message. 'They'll all be outside, working. Can I have your keys, Mother? I'll nip down in the car.'

Leonie drove as fast as she dared down the steep, winding lane to Springfield Farm, and drew up in the yard to a welcoming chorus from the farm dogs. Chris Morgan emerged from a barn, wiping oily hands on a rag.

'Haven't seen him, Leo, but I've been in here, wrestling with a tractor,' he said in response to her urgent enquiry. 'I'll tell everyone to keep their eyes peeled for him. He can't be far.'

'Thanks, Chris. I'll search through the lanes, see if I can spot him anywhere.' She pulled a face. 'I just hope I can find him before Fenny gets home.'

Leonie drove slowly through the interlinking lanes round the farm, but there was no sign of a frisking yellow dog. Eventually she gave up and drove back to Friars Wood, praying Marzi would be there to greet her when she got in.

'No sign?' said her mother anxiously. 'Where on earth can he have gone?'

'Ring the police, while I go out in the garden again,' said Leonie. 'Better safe than sorry. Someone might have seen him, or picked him up, even.'

'Right,' said Frances briskly. 'I'll ring the vet, too. They put notices up in the surgery.'

Leonie thrust a hand through her hair. 'You don't think he could have fallen down the cliff, do you, Mother?'

'I admit the idea haunts me! Though why he should do that now, all of a sudden, I can't imagine.'

'I'll grab some hiking boots and drive up the road this time,' said Leonie. 'I'll park the car at the viewing point and climb down to search the river path. I've got my phone, so if I find him I can always ring for help.'

'For heaven's sake be careful,' said Frances, looking worried. 'Perhaps I should ring your father—'

'Wait until I've looked everywhere first. No point in worrying him unnecessarily.' Leonie ran upstairs for the boots. She braided her hair swiftly and secured the end with a rubber band, then went down to the study to collect her father's binoculars. 'What did they say?' she asked as she joined her mother in the kitchen.

'No one has reported him, but the constable put me on to the dog warden, who took the details and promised to keep a look-out. Next I'll spread the word at all the local vets.' Frances kissed her suddenly. 'As I said, be careful. Please.'

Leonie collected Marzi's lead, then went out to drive a mile or so up the road to the easiest point to climb down to the riverbed. It was a long time since she'd done anything so energetic, and though the way down was a fairly easy scramble compared to the sheer cliffs below Friars Wood, she was hot and breathless by the time she slithered down the last few feet to the river. She sat down on a boulder for a moment to get her breath back, thankful it was a fine day. Heavy rain would have made her search ten times more difficult, even impossible, if the path was as demanding as she remembered. She soon found that it was even more so. Obliterated in places by fallen stones and boulders, in others thick with undergrowth, it was as much as she could do to get past at some points. And because she stopped every few minutes to whistle and call, and scan the area with the binoculars, the going was slow. Leonie waited every time, hoping to hear barking in response. But when she reached the point below Brockhill, where there was no way through, she was forced to admit defeat.

She made even slower progress on the return journey, her mind full of hearbreaking pictures of the dog lying unconscious somewhere, with no means of getting back home. She was breathless and weary by the time she'd climbed back up to the car, and, hoping against hope that Marzi might have turned up in the meantime, she drove home.

One look at her mother's face was enough. 'I saw no sign of him,' reported Leonie miserably.

'At least *you're* safe,' said Frances, with a thankful sigh. 'Chris Morgan rang to say they've searched everywhere on the farm, but with no luck. I suppose we should be thankful Marzi didn't get in with the sheep.'

Leonie thought of the old gate she'd wrenched open on her way to Brockhill. 'There's one place I haven't checked,' she said reluctantly, and told her mother about her scramble along the overgrown path on her way to see Jonah the night before.

'You went along that dangerous old path in the *dark?*' said her mother, horrified. 'I thought you'd gone up the road when Jonah said he'd drive you back. Were you mad, child?'

'I didn't realise it was such an obstacle course these days,' said Leonie sheepishly.

'Now Brockhill is empty your father keeps it that way on purpose as a security measure,' said Frances severely. 'You say the gate is off its hinges?'

'They'd rusted away. The latch was the only thing keeping it in place.' Leonie heaved a sigh. 'I suppose

I'd better check in case Marzi's got himself stuck along there somewhere.'

'For heaven's sake be careful you don't slip after that heavy rain!'

When she set out along the path behind the Stables Leonie could hardly credit her recklessness at storming along it in the dark. In daylight it was revealed as a narrow, dangerously uneven track at the very edge of the cliff, as slippery as melted chocolate now, with overgrown bushes at intervals as the only barrier between the unwary and the precipitous drop below.

Appalled at the thought of what could have happened in the dark, Leonie placed her feet with great care, peering down the cliff every few minutes for any sign of the dog. Her heart was in her mouth as she lost her footing more than once before the track turned inland towards Brockhill and the rusty old gate, which lay where she'd left it in the undergrowth. And all her calling and whistling was in vain. There was no sign of Marzi by the time she left Friars Wood land and came out on Brockhill property. Leonie emerged into the old walled garden at last, certain the dog wouldn't have come this far, but apprehensive about going back the way she'd come. She decided to sneak down the drive past the lodge, and hope Jonah was too busy to notice.

But when she reached the open lawns he was the first person she saw, and her first instinct was to turn tail and race back the way she'd come no matter what. Jonah was in deep discussion with a man who was gazing intently at the roof, but to her dismay he spotted her at once, and left his companion to walk towards her.

'Miss Dysart, good day,' he said loudly. 'What can I do for you?' As he came close, out of earshot, he frowned. 'What's wrong, Leo? You look terrible.'

At the unlooked for concern in his voice Leonie wanted to hurl herself into his arms. Instead she greeted him politely, and told him the dog was missing. 'I've looked everywhere,' she said breathlessly. 'Along the river, and down to the farm, all through the lanes. Then I came back here along the old path again just in case—' She broke off, flushing. 'But you're busy, and I'm holding you up. I trespassed this far because I couldn't face going back along the path. In daylight it's a lot more terrifying than I remembered it. Heaven knows how I managed to make it along there in the dark. I meant to skirt the house and go down the drive to the road.'

'Without seeing me?'

'Yes.' The colour deepened in her flushed, sweating face. 'I thought you'd prefer that.'

Jonah glanced back at the house. 'The architect's about to leave, anyway. Hang on a minute, and I'll drive you back.'

'No, please,' said Leonie, recoiling. 'I can walk.'

'No, you can't,' he said firmly. 'You look exhausted. Come with me. Once John Parkhouse has gone I'll take you back.'

With formality Jonah introduced her as Miss Dysart of Friars Wood, and the architect, a pleasant man in his fifties, shook her hand and told her he knew her father well, then with a word to Jonah about a return visit later in the week, he got in his car and drove off.

'Right, let's go,' said Jonah, 'unless you'd like some coffee first?'

'No, thanks. Mother's probably picturing me in pieces down on the rocks.'

'As well she might,' observed Jonah grimly, as he helped her into the seat. 'How long has the dog been gone?'

'Dad took him out first thing this morning, and left him foraging in the wood as usual. It was only when I decided to take Marzi for a walk that we realised he was missing.' Leonie bit her lip. 'He always comes straight in for his breakfast.'

'He's bound to turn up,' said Jonah firmly.

'If so I wish he'd put a move on, and preferably before Fenny gets home from school while he's at it,' said Leonie with feeling. 'He was her Christmas present two years ago, so she called him Marzipan, because of his coat. She adores him.'

Jonah put a hand out to touch hers fleetingly. 'I'll help you look.'

Frances Dysart greeted them with relief, taking Jonah's presence in her stride. 'I was beginning to think you were lost as well, Leo,' she said, filling a kettle. 'You'll stay to lunch, Jonah?'

He shot a look at Leonie. 'I don't—'

'It's no big deal, just soup,' said Frances briskly. 'Leonie, I suggest you wash your face first.'

Leonie did as she was told, and found she was a mess. Bits of leaf and twig were caught in her hair and her face was streaked with mud and sweat, even blood in one place from a scratch. Roberto wouldn't have recognised her. But Jonah had preferred her untidy. Once upon a time. He had always liked her early-morning face more than the one she presented to the world. It had been one of life's greatest pleasures to wake to Jonah's caressing eyes... She took in a deep, bracing breath, brushed hard at the hair she'd released from its braid, then touched a lipstick to her mouth and went downstairs to sit opposite Jonah at the kitchen table. Something she'd never expected to happen again.

'I thought I might climb down the cliff after lunch

and take a look round,' said Jonah, accepting a bowl of soup.

Leonie eyed him in alarm. 'What if you fall?'

'You hang out over the Eyrie balustrade, phone in hand, ready to call for help,' he said matter-of-factly. 'But I won't fall. I do a bit of amateur mountaineering these day, when I have the time.'

Frances Dysart frowned anxiously. 'That's very kind of you, Jonah, but I wouldn't want you to take risks.'

'There's no other way down to search below the property,' he pointed out. 'If nothing else I can make sure poor Marzi's not marooned down there somewhere, with no means of getting up.'

Leonie grimaced, picturing the dog's distress only too vividly. 'Thanks, Jonah. It's very kind of you.'

'The Eyrie's the ideal spot. I can secure the rope round the stone balustrade, and go down from there,' he said briskly. 'After lunch I'll go back to the house for rope.'

Later, with Tom Dysart's powerful binoculars slung round his neck, Jonah secured the rope to the balustrade, then swung himself over the edge and smiled reassuringly at Leonie as he braced himself for the descent.

'Watch your step,' she said sternly, brandishing her phone at him. 'And remember—one slip and I use this.'

He grinned, then pushed with his feet and abseiled out in an arc that took Leonie's breath away. She heard him grunt as his feet made contact with the cliff face again, then he continued downwards in the same way until he had no more rope to play with. She hung out as far as she could, then to her relief heard him shout.

'I've found a foothold on a ledge, Leo. I can't go any

further, so I'll take a look through the glasses before I come back up.'

Leonie waited, tense, as she heard him whistling and shouting, waiting, then whistling again. At last he called. 'Leo? There's no sign of him anywhere.'

'Then for heaven's sake come back up,' she yelled.

Jonah's progress back up the cliff was so much slower than his descent Leo's heart was in her mouth the entire time as the rope creaked and groaned with his weight as he made his way up towards the Eyrie, pausing here and there to negotiate the shrubs and bushes which clung to the cliff face. Then to Leonie's horror there was a sudden fall of stones and shale, followed by blood-curdling silence.

'Jonah. *Jonah!*' she screamed, hanging out as far as she could.

'Still here,' he called faintly. 'No need for an SOS—yet.'

Leonie felt she'd lived through several hours by the time Jonah came into view. She gasped as she saw his bloodstained face, and once his shoulders appeared seized him by the upper arms and heaved with all her might, to such effect that they both sprawled full length together on the stone floor of the Eyrie. With a muttered curse Jonah heaved himself upright.

'Don't touch your face; you might infect it,' said Leonie, scrambling to her knees. She dug into her jeans pockets for a tissue, but without success. 'Come on, move, we'd better get you to the house.'

'I'll come, but not quickly,' he panted. 'I'm out of condition. I hadn't bargained on a mini-avalanche in my face.'

She jumped up, offering a hand to help him, and Jonah took it, swaying a little as he stood upright. 'Come on,' she urged. 'Leave the rope. Let's get that face seen to.'

Jonah grimaced, then swore as blood poured down his face. 'Damn,' he said bitterly. 'I heard a noise and like a fool looked up just as the stones came down. Normally I wear a helmet, but I didn't have one with me. My nose took the worst of it, hence the blood.'

'I'm to blame for letting you go down there in the first place,' she retorted, and put her arm through his to support him as she hurried him back along the path. 'Hurry up, Jonah, you're bleeding like a stuck pig.'

He let out a stifled laugh, then paled suddenly, wrenched his arm free and bent to throw up behind a bush. Leonie walked tactfully on, and waited for him to catch up with her.

'Sorry about that,' he apologised, ashen-faced.

Leonie took his arm again, literally hauling him along towards the house. 'Come *on*,' she said urgently. 'Mother's an old hand at treating wounds.'

Frances Dysart exclaimed in horror at Jonah's face, then went straight into paramedic mode. She cleansed his face and clapped a bag of frozen peas to his nose. 'Put some ice in a proper bag, Leo, then take Jonah off to the hospital,' she pronounced when she'd finished.

Jonah shook his head, then gasped in pain, regretting it. 'I don't need—'

'Yes, you do,' retorted Leonie, her pallor matching his. 'Your nose could be broken.'

'She's right,' said Frances firmly. 'And you may be concussed, too. Best to be sure, Jonah.'

In her desperate haste to get Jonah to the Community Hospital Leonie demanded the keys to his car, which was blocking her mother's. She helped him up into it, then hauled herself into the driver's seat, switched on the ignition, and backed along the terrace with extreme caution until she was able to turn in front of the Stables. Once they were on the main road she felt more confident, and, after a muffled request from behind Jonah's ice-pack to move to the left-hand side of the road, made it to the Community Hospital without further mishap. It was only after Jonah had been taken away for treatment that Leonie began to suffer reaction, as she assured a nurse that the large stain down her yellow sweater was someone else's blood, not her own.

Jonah was returned to her after an X-ray, complete with a large plaster across his nose and a black scowl.

'Nothing broken, and he's not actually concussed, but Mr Savage must stay in bed until tomorrow. He can't drive for a day or two,' reported the nurse. 'But after that he should be fine.'

'Did the woman think my injury had deprived me of speech?' demanded Jonah irritably as they went out to the car.

Leonie smiled sweetly. 'No. She suspected—correctly—that your male ego wouldn't let you mention concussion and enforced rest and so on.'

'Fat chance of a male ego flourishing in your vicinity,' he snapped, and spurned her help to get into the car.

When Leonie turned up, very carefully, into the winding drive of Friars Wood Jonah's scowled deepened. 'I thought you were taking me to Brockhill.'

'In your condition?' she said scornfully. 'Don't be silly.'

'I am perfectly capable of putting myself to bed!'

'Do you *have* a bed at the lodge?'

'When I stay there I sleep on the sofa-bed in the room I'm using as an office,' he said stiffly.

The sofa where he'd conducted his little experiment, thought Leonie, teeth clenched at the memory.

'Otherwise,' he added, 'I stay at the company flat over the Pennington offices.'

'No driving, so that's out of the question,' she informed him. 'Stay there—I'll come round and give you a hand.'

Jonah ignored her and got out unaided, then slumped against the car, looking ghastly.

'Oh, for heaven's sake,' said Leonie impatiently, and took him by the arm. 'Come on. Mother will want to know how you got on. And I promised to fetch Kate and Fenny. Can I borrow your car?'

'Would I dare refuse?' he gasped. 'But for God's sake drive on the left.'

Leonie ignored the taunt, eyeing his greenish pallor with concern as she supported him up the path to the front door. 'Feeling sick?'

'No,' he lied, sweat beading his clenched mouth.

Frances came to meet them, eyeing Jonah anxiously. She listened to Leonie's report, then took the invalid by the arm. 'Kate rang to say she's staying the night with Laura to revise together, so if you'll pick Fenny up I'll see to Jonah.'

'If I could just sit down for a bit,' he said unevenly, 'perhaps you'd be good enough to run me up to Brockhill when you get back, Leo.'

Frances made soothing noises as she installed him in a comfortable chair in the study. 'Just take it easy for a while, Jonah.'

Leonie stood looking at him for a moment, then saw her mother eyeing her bloodstained front. 'I'll change before I go,' she said swiftly. 'See you later, Jonah.'

'Right,' he muttered, without opening his eyes. 'Sorry about this.'

'Nonsense,' said Frances briskly. 'You were looking for our dog, remember? I'll make some tea,' she added, and went out.

Leonie touched Jonah's hand. 'How do you feel? Truthfully, I mean.'

'Confused,' he murmured, then his eyes opened to look straight up into hers. 'For a moment, back there in the Eyrie, Leo, I could have sworn you cared.'

'Of course I cared,' she said, flushing. 'It was my dog, I felt responsible.'

'Of course.' His jaw tightened. 'Talking of the dog, what are you going to tell Fenny?'

'The truth, I suppose.'

'Poor little mite. She'll be devastated.'

'I know,' said Leonie miserably.

Jonah's eyes hardened to green ice. 'At least he didn't leave a note, telling her he didn't want her any more.'

Leonie glared at him. 'You just couldn't resist it, could you? Does it give you a buzz to turn the knife?'

'You bet it does. I'm only human, Leonie Dysart.'

'So am I!'

'Really?' He closed his eyes wearily. 'You could have fooled me.'

CHAPTER EIGHT

As EXPECTED, Fenny was inconsolable when Leonie told her, as gently as she could, that the dog was missing. She cried most of the way home in the car, her only ray of light in the gloom the prospect of Jonah waiting to see her. To make it clear that everything possible was being done to find her beloved Marzi, Leonie described her search along the riverbed, and in glowing terms described Jonah's bravery in abseiling down the cliff.

'The thing is, Fen,' she said, as she drew up outside the house, 'Marzi is probably playing with another dog somewhere right this minute, having far too good a time to come home. He'll be back soon. You'll see.'

Fenny was unconvinced, and rushed to hurl herself at Frances when they went into the house. Once she'd calmed down and taken off her hat and blazer, Fenny looked round her, frowning, the striking green eyes meeting Leonie's in accusation.

'You said Jonah was here!'

'He is,' Frances assured her. 'But he's in bed in Jess's room. He hurt his head when he was climbing up the cliff, so I put him to bed.'

Leonie gazed at her in awe. 'How on earth did you manage that?'

'I was nice to him,' said her mother simply. Her lips twitched. 'And to be honest I think Jonah was feeling so terrible by that stage he was beyond argument.'

'Can I go and see him?' said Fenny eagerly.

'He's sleeping at the moment, sweetheart. You can

see him after you've had some tea and done your home-work.'

The little girl sighed, then looked hopefully at Leonie. 'I've got sums tonight—will you help me, Leo?'

It was a severe lesson in discipline for Leonie to sit at the kitchen table and drink tea with her mother, and try to reassure a very forlorn Fenny about the dog, when all the time every instinct was urging her to race upstairs to check on Jonah. Fool to think she was over him. Seven years or seventy, it obviously made no difference. All this time, far away in Italy, she'd been deluding her-self, sure that her love for him had died the day she'd heard him with Rachel. But believing, for one horrifying moment, that he'd fallen down the cliff had set her straight once and for all.

'In a minute, Leo, while Fenny does her homework, you can go up very quietly and see if Jonah would like something to drink,' said Frances briskly. 'And at the same time ask him if he's up to receiving a little visitor.'

'All right,' said Leonie, elaborately casual as she made herself collect the cups and take the tray over to the sink first. Then she met her mother's eye and saw that her act was a wash-out. She smiled sheepishly, and promised Fenny to help with the sums when she got back. 'Though I'm sure a clever girl like you can do them on her own, really.'

Upstairs, Leo tapped quietly on Jess's door and went in.

Jonah lay with eyes closed, propped up on frilly pil-lows which made an incongruous background for his bare, muscular shoulders. Bruises were coming up fast round his eyes, startling against the pallor of his face. Leonie tiptoed across to the bed, then halted as his eyes opened and looked straight into hers, transporting her straight back to the last time they had occupied a bedroom together. Heat rose in her face as the look in Jonah's eyes told her he was remembering the same thing.

'How are you feeling?' she asked, deliberately formal.

'Guilty for causing so much trouble.' His mouth twisted. 'My aim was help, not hindrance.'

'You're lucky you didn't fall and break your neck,' she said severely, seized by a sudden longing to climb in beside him.

'True,' he acknowledged. 'But in the end I didn't even break my nose. I don't suppose the dog has made it back home yet?'

Leonie sighed. 'Afraid not. But Fenny has, and she wants to see you. Are you up for it?'

'Of course.' He smiled gingerly. 'I hope my face won't frighten her.'

'No way. Wounded hero, and all that. You were top of her list before, but now you've risked life and limb to find Marzi she's your slave for ever!'

'I just wish my efforts had been successful—and caused less commotion,' he added irritably.

'We're very grateful,' Leonie assured him. 'By the way, you must have something to drink. What would you like?'

'I would *like* to get up and relieve you of my troublesome presence,' said Jonah caustically, then winced as he levered himself higher.

'Since you can't even move without causing yourself pain that's hardly a practical requirement,' she retorted then her eyes softened. 'Does your head hurt?'

'Like hell,' he admitted, swallowing.

'Right,' said Leonie, making for the door. 'I'll fetch

some mild painkillers and something to wash it down with. I'll tell Fenny not to stay long.'

When Leonie returned with a tray, Fenny was perched on the end of the bed, discussing the dog's disappearance. 'Perhaps Marzi's gone off to live with some other little girl,' she said forlornly.

'Not a chance; he belongs to you,' said Jonah firmly. 'He's probably lost his way, and someone will find him, and either bring him home or take him to the police station.'

Fenny climbed down off the bed disconsolately. 'I wish he'd come home soon. It's getting dark and he'll be cold.' She brightened suddenly. 'Mummy says you're going to sleep here tonight, Jonah.'

He shot a startled look at Leonie, who nodded in confirmation as she poured mineral water into a glass. 'That's right. Jonah's head hurts, Fenny, so we're going to keep him here until he's better.'

'Goody!' Fenny cheered up considerably. 'When I come up to bed I'll read you a story, Jonah,' she offered.

'I'd like that very much,' he assured her, looking rather white around the mouth.

'Run down and finish your sums, darling,' said Leonie, 'and I'll be down in a minute to check.'

Fenny gave the invalid a very careful kiss on the cheek, thanked him earnestly for his efforts to find her dog, then with reluctance trailed off to finish her homework.

'I thought my stay in bed was a temporary arrangement,' muttered Jonah.

'You can't drive,' Leonie reminded him, giving him some pills. 'And suppose I drove you back to Brockhill? Can you see my mother allowing you to go back to that comfortless lodge, with no proper bed and no one to look after you?'

Jonah washed the pills down with most of the water, then lay back on the pillows, looking haggard. 'Put like that, Leo, no, I can't.' He gave her a brooding look. 'You must be heartily sorry you made it home for the party, all things considered.'

'Of course not. I'm glad I was here for Adam,' she said quickly. 'I'm even more glad I know the truth about Rachel. As you said the other night, it's too late to mend things between you and me, but I'd like to think we can be friends.'

'Oh, hell!' Jonah tensed, his breathing suddenly rapid. 'Leo—out of the way, please, I'm going to be sick.' He slid out of bed and ran for the bathroom across the landing.

Leonie tidied the bed while he was out of the room, then waited until he staggered back.

'Never mind getting back to Brockhill, I ought to take you back to the hospital and tell them to keep you in for observation,' she warned, as she helped him into bed.

'Not a chance!' Jonah lay shivering, eyeing her with bitter hostility. 'I think you're enjoying this.'

'Certainly not,' she retorted. 'Do you feel dizzy?'

'No,' he said firmly. 'I no longer feel sick, I am not dizzy, and I have no intention of going back to the hospital!'

'All right, keep your hair on.' Leonie tidied the covers briskly. 'You've lost your painkillers, I suppose, but you'd better hang on a while before taking any more. Drink more water. Lots of it.'

'Yes, Nurse,' he said wearily, and closed his eyes.

'That's right,' she said in approval. 'Try to sleep.'

*   *   *

When Tom Dysart came home Fenny was full of Marzi's disappearance, the tragedy of it mitigated for her only slightly by the presence of Jonah Dysart in Jess's bed. By the time Tom had heard the full story of Leonie's search, Jonah's ill-fated climb down the cliff and checked with his wife that all authorities possible had been contacted about the missing dog, it was time for Fenny to go to bed.

'I'll take you up tonight, sweetheart,' he said. 'Then we can call in on Jonah so I can thank him.'

'Ask him how he feels, and if he fancies some dinner later,' said Frances. 'If he's not in the mood for roast chicken, offer scrambled eggs.'

Jonah's presence upstairs in her sister's bed made the evening difficult for Leonie, though he had declined all offers of food, other than some biscuits to drink with the tea Frances took up to him after the meal.

'He looks ghastly,' she reported when she returned to the study. 'Though I suppose he got off lightly in the circumstance. He could have gone crashing to the foot of the cliff.'

A thought which had haunted Leonie all evening, interfering with her enthusism for dinner. 'And after all that effort the dog's still missing,' she said with a sigh. 'Poor Fenny.'

'He's bound to turn up,' said her father firmly. 'Someone will find him and bring him back.'

'He's a pedigree, though,' said Frances, looking worried. 'Do you think he could have been stolen?'

It was a thought which added to Leonie's restless night later. She called in on Jonah on the way to bed, secretly disappointed to find him asleep. She stood looking down at his bruised face for a time, then turned off the bedside lamp and went to check on a sleeping Fenny, her heart wrung at the sight of the flushed, tearstained little face.

Men and dogs, thought Leonie morosely. No point in giving your heart to either life form; it only gets hurt at some time or other.

During the night she surfaced from a restless doze, wondering what had disturbed her. Then she shot upright at the sound of muffled sobbing, and leapt out of bed to run to Fenny's room, pulling on a dressing gown as she went.

'Darling, don't,' she said, gathering the little girl in her arms. 'You'll make yourself ill.'

'I was dreaming,' wept Fenny, clutching at Leonie.

'Was it a bad dream?'

'No—a lovely dream. Marzi was p-p-playing with me in the garden, but then I woke up and I *remembered*...' Fenny sobbed bitterly, and Leonie held her close and rocked her in her arms until she was quiet.

It took a drink of water, a visit to the bathroom and a lot of cuddling before Leonie was able to settle the distraught Fenny back to sleep. Afterwards she went back along the landing to find Jonah propped in Jess's doorway, arrayed in the dressing gown her father kept for holidays.

'What's wrong?' he whispered. 'Is she ill?'

Leonie drew him inside the room and shut the door as she explained. 'Don't let her hear you—it took me quite a while to settle her back. Are you all right? Do you want more pills?'

Jonah slumped down on a chair. 'Thirst's more my problem than headache right now. I've finished everything your mother left for me. I was about to take my glass to the bathroom tap when I heard you.'

'I'll get you another bottle of mineral water. Stay here, and don't move until I get back,' she ordered. 'If you pass out on the floor I don't fancy lugging you back into bed.'

Jonah gave her a hostile look, but stayed where he was, more because he felt too rotten to get up, Leonie could tell, rather than obedience to her instructions. When she returned, he was standing up, swaying so ominously she pushed him down on the bed impatiently.

'For heaven's sake sit there and be sensible, Jonah.' She poured water into a glass and gave it to him. 'Drink that.'

'Yes, Nurse,' he muttered, and drained the glass thirstily, looking drawn and haggard, the plaster on his nose startlingly white against his rapidly blackening eyes.

'Let me help you off with that,' she said briskly, as he stood up to take off the dressing gown.

'Don't worry, I'm quite respectable underneath,' he assured her, and sat down rather suddenly on the edge of the bed. 'Your mother gave me a pair of Adam's pyjama trousers. Pristine and unworn, she told me.'

'I didn't know he had any,' said Leonie, smiling a little. She eyed him uneasily. 'Will you be all right now, Jonah?'

'I'll be fine. Go to bed, Leo, you look tired.'

'It's been quite a day,' she pointed out. 'Action-packed, and pretty scary at times.'

'Sorry I added to the strain,' he said sombrely. 'I just wish we'd been able to find the dog.'

'So do I,' she said unsteadily, visited by a sudden desire to cry her eyes out, just like Fenny.

'Come here,' Jonah ordered, patting the bed.

Leonie slumped down beside him, shoulders hunched as she fished in her pocket for a tissue. 'Sorry,' she said thickly.

Jonah put a careful arm round her. 'Even big girls cry, Leo.'

She scrubbed fiercely at her eyes. 'I know. In Italy they say *"piangi"* at times like these. No one ever says "don't cry".'

'Ah, yes. Italy.' He removed his arm. 'A timely reminder. Wouldn't do to poach on someone else's preserves.'

She turned to glare at him. 'I'm not a pot of jam!'

'True.' His eyes gleamed as they met hers. 'Honey, maybe?' he countered softly, in a tone which made her toes curl.

Leonie stared, hypnotised, her heart thudding at the memory of Jonah's passion for honey. When they'd shared breakfast in bed that last day together traces of it had lingered on his mouth afterwards, his caressing lips leaving stickiness on her breasts he'd taken so tormentingly long to lick away she'd been crazy for him by the time he'd finally made love to her. She saw Jonah's eyes kindle, knew he was sharing the same memory, and suddenly it was hard to breathe.

Jonah leaned nearer, and very slowly drew her into his arms and cradled her against him, his breath catching as she melted, unresisting, against him. In contrast to his punitive kisses at Brockhill, Jonah's lips touched hers with the merest feather of contact, the tip of his tongue tracing the outline of her mouth before his lips settled on hers, deeping the pressure, and her mouth opened in the old, familiar response she had never been able to control.

'I was right,' he whispered against her mouth. 'Pure, irresistible honey.'

Leonie shivered as he pushed the robe aside to caress her through the thin cotton jersey of her nightshirt. She gasped as her nipples stood up in peaks to his touch, then Jonah's mouth was on hers in demand, and they fell back on the bed together, kissing wildly as his hands slid beneath the nightshirt to trace the outline of her hips before settling on them to hold her hard against him.

'We shouldn't be doing this—' she whispered back.

'Because your lover would object?' he demanded harshly.

Leonie stiffened. Roberto had never entered her mind. 'Not that. Though he would, of course. But you're injured, remember.' Angry with herself for losing control, she detached herself and stood up, tying the sash of her robe viciously tight. 'Besides, you made it very clear the other night that it's too late for anything like this between us.'

Jonah's bruised eyes turned to ice. 'Good of you to remind me. My thanks for the ministering angel act, Leonie. But your bedside manner could use some work. Goodnight. I won't disturb you again.'

He was wrong about that, she thought miserably, as she got back into bed. It was disturbing to be in the same country with Jonah, let alone having him in the same house, with only a bedroom wall to separate them. Leonie lay looking out at the stars, thankful she'd pulled herself together before making a complete fool of herself. For a mad, abandoned moment she'd forgotten that her parents and Fenny were sleeping nearby, forgotten Roberto, and everything else other than the bliss of being held close in Jonah's arms again. His injury had been the only thing to keep her from surrendering unconditionally. And to a man who said it was too late for anything between them. She thumped her pillow in frustration. The chemistry between them was as powerful as ever, but not enough, it was obvious, to make up to him for her rejection.

CHAPTER NINE

NEXT morning Leonie was up at first light, hoping against hope that Marzi had made his way back. She peeped in on a sleeping Jonah, then ran downstairs to open the scullery door, her heart sinking when she found no sign of a panting, hungry dog waiting to be let in. She pulled on boots and a jacket and went on a protracted tour of the gardens and the wood, but in the end gave up and trudged back to the house to prepare breakfast.

After the first urgent enquiry about her beloved pet Fenny was very subdued, refusing to eat, and unwilling afterwards to go to school. 'I want to stay home and look for Marzi,' she said truculently.

It took a great deal of tact and firmness from the others before she gave in and put on her blazer and raincoat.

'I'll drive you to school this morning, sweetheart,' said Frances, swallowing a second cup of tea. 'I need some shopping.'

'In that case I'll get off,' said Tom, kissing all his womenfolk in turn. 'I could do with an early start today. See you tonight.'

'Can I go up and say goodbye to Jonah before I go?' demanded Fenny.

'Go very quietly, but if he's still asleep don't wake him. Jonah's not very well, remember,' warned Frances. 'But if he is awake, ask him if he's hungry.'

'He was fast asleep when I got up,' Leonie reported.

'You obviously had a bad night,' said her mother after

the little girl hurried off. 'Fenny told me about her dream. I heard you go to her so I left you to it, especially when I heard Jonah's voice.'

'He was thirsty,' said Leonie, avoiding her mother's eye. 'I went down to get him some mineral water.'

'He's probably hungry, too, by this time, so I'll leave you to cook whatever he wants, Leo.' Frances smiled wryly. 'I actually do need some shopping, but my real reason for the school run is to tell Fenny's teacher about the dog. She's liable to have a concentration problem today.'

Fenny came running in to say Jonah was awake. 'He said he didn't want anything, Mummy,' she said, looking worried. 'But I told him he had to eat, or he wouldn't get better.'

'Quite right, too,' approved Frances.

'I'll go and see him in a minute,' said Leonie, and gave Fenny a kiss. 'Have you got your homework? I'll come for you this afternoon, sweetheart.'

Something in the way her mother said goodbye told Leonie she was leaving her daughter alone with Jonah for a purpose, in the hope that sheer propinquity might bring them together again. Secretly Leonie shared the hope. In your dreams, dearie, she scoffed, and went upstairs to enquire after the invalid.

Jonah was standing by the window in his dressing gown. When he turned Leonie saw he'd washed as much of his face as he could and tidied his hair, neither of which did much to detract from the piratical effect of a day's growth of stubble which toned well with his black eyes.

'Good morning,' she greeted him, determinedly cheerful. 'How do you feel?'

'Much better,' he assured her, unsmiling. 'I would have dressed, but my clothes are missing.'

'You bled copiously over us both, so Mother washed everything last night. Your things are dry now,' she added. 'You can have them after breakfast.'

'I'll pass on breakfast, if you don't mind—'

'I do mind,' she retorted. 'Besides, I hear Fenny's already issued instructions about eating.'

Jonah's eyes softened. 'True. But I've given your mother trouble enough already, so if you'll just give me my clothes I'll get off to Brockhill and have breakfast there. Alone,' he added.

'Mother isn't here. And when she gets back from her shopping I, for one, don't fancy greeting her with the news that you've absconded.' Leonie looked him in the eye. 'After all, it wouldn't be the first time we've breakfasted together.'

Jonah's jaw tightened. 'I'll accept some toast and coffee, if only to please your mother,' he said with chill courtesy. 'But I prefer to dress first.'

'Whatever,' she said carelessly. 'I'll fetch your clothes. I can even supply you with a razor.'

When Jonah finally joined her in the kitchen, minus stubble and attired in clean khaki trousers and white shirt, Leonie waved him to a chair and pushed a full toast rack towards him.

'The marmalade's home-made,' she informed him.

Jonah surveyed the table then brought his eyes up very deliberately to meet hers. 'No honey?' he said silkily.

'Afraid not,' she returned, unruffled. 'Would you like the morning paper?' she added briskly, as she passed his cup.

'Thank you. Just the property section will do.'

They sat with newspapers propped in front of them

like shields. For all the world like an old married couple after a flaming row, thought Leonie glumly. Eventually Jonah put his paper down and asked for more coffee.

'How do you intend to spend your time while you're home?' he asked politely.

'Looking for the dog again today, I suppose. I thought I'd go out in the car, cover as much ground as possible.'

'After my fiasco, I'd advise keeping your search to safe territory.'

'I will.' She scrutinised his face. 'Tell me the truth, are you really feeling better, Jonah?'

He smiled fleetingly. 'My appetite's back, so I must be. Wonderful bread.'

'Mother makes it herself.' Leonie handed over the toast rack. 'Have some more.'

'Thank you.' He eyed her plate. 'You haven't eaten much.'

'I rarely eat much breakfast.'

'You used to, once upon a time,' he reminded her. Their eyes met.

'Not any more,' she said quietly, and refilled her cup. Jonah finished eating before he spoke again. 'You know, Leo, I've been thinking over something you said last night.'

She eyed him narrowly. 'What, exactly?'

'That we could at least be friends.'

'Oh. Right.' She'd actually *said* that? Anyone would think she'd had the knock on the head, not Jonah. She didn't want to be 'friends'. She wanted what she'd had before. And thrown away.

'You don't sound enthusiastic,' he commented.

Leonie looked at him levelly. 'Is that what you want?'

'It would certainly be more convenient.'

Convenient!

'In what way?' she asked coolly.

'I shall be based at Pennington for the time being, and you'll be home for a while.' He paused, and Leonie held her breath. 'Now everything's out in the open I'd like to see more of Fenny while I'm involved at Brockhill. It would be easier all round if you and I were on speaking terms, Leo.'

Easier for whom? thought Leonie, shaken. If his sole object in visiting Friars Wood was to see Fenny, Jonah had his revenge in full. 'Of course. Come as often as you like. I shan't be here all the time, anyway,' she added with sudden inspiration. 'I'm going to stay with Jess for a day or two.' Which would be news to Jess.

'The call of the bright lights?'

'Something like that.' Leonie stood up. 'Look, I can see you're champing at the bit. I'll tell Mother you ate breakfast, so by all means take off for Brockhill now, if you want.'

'I do,' he said promptly, getting to his feet. 'Give my thanks to your mother. You've all been very kind.'

'The least we could do in the circumstances,' Leonie assured him, and walked with him to the door.

'Let me know if the dog comes back, Leo,' Jonah told her. 'If he doesn't maybe your parents will let me take Fenny out for the day while you're in London. Distract her a little.'

'I'm sure they'd be delighted. Fenny most of all.' She opened the door and smiled brightly. 'Take care, Jonah, don't overdo it.'

He gave her a searching look. 'Leo, before I go there's something else. Now the secret's out, I'd very much like to tell my parents the truth about Fenny.' He smiled bleakly. 'My mother tends to lecture me about her lack of grandchildren, so acquaintance with Fenny would be a great bonus for her. And for my father. They were both very fond of Rachel.'

'Will they feel the same way when they discover she was Richard's mistress?' said Leonie bluntly, and had the satisfaction of seeing Jonah wince.

'I shall explain the situation, naturally,' he snapped.

'Before you do you'd better consult Mother and Dad.'

'I intend to. But you were my first concern, Leo.'

'Thank you. But your parents ought to know, anyway.' She bit her lip. 'Jonah, were they very angry with me after—after I broke up with you?'

His smile was sardonic. 'Not at all. They were angry with *me*, convinced I was to blame. My protestations met with total disbelief.'

'No!' Leonie stared at him in dismay. 'Jonah, I'm so *sorry*. It never occurred to me that you'd get the blame. I always wished I could give some kind of explanation. They were very kind to me,' she added sadly.

'Then you can understand why I'd like to tell them what really happened.'

'Of course. Would you like me to ask Mother and Dad, or would you prefer to bring it up with them yourself?'

'The latter, if you don't mind. And sooner, rather than later.'

Leonie nodded. 'Come over for a drink after Dad gets home. You can see Fenny at the same time and assure her you're still alive.'

Jonah smiled wryly. 'I'm inflicting my presence on your family to an extraordinary extent lately.'

'They won't mind at all,' she assured him. 'They're only too happy to welcome you here, Jonah.'

'Do you agree with them, Leo?'

She nodded. 'Of course. Now I know the truth.'

There was silence for a moment, then Jonah looked at his watch and whistled softly. 'I must be off. I'll find a list of messages a mile long. I'll see you later, then. About seven?'

'Fine. But don't overdo it,' she added. 'And mind you eat some lunch.'

'Yes, Nurse!'

Visited by a sudden fierce longing to ask Jonah to stay, Leonie watched him back the car along the terrace, then went indoors to clear away while she waited for her mother to get home. When Frances came in, laden with grocery bags, Leonie passed on Jonah's thanks and asked for the car keys so she could go off to look for Marzi.

'You never know, I might be lucky.'

Frances nodded glumly. 'I hope so. I think I'll ring the dog warden again.'

'By the way,' said Leonie, on her way to the door. 'Jonah has a question to put to you and Dad, so I suggested he came round about seven for a drink.'

'Does that mean—?'

'No, it doesn't. He wants me for a friend, now, not a wife.'

'Oh, dear.' Her mother's face fell. 'And what do you want, darling?'

'I want him back,' said Leonie with sudden passion. 'But Jonah's made it clear that Fenny's the attraction in this household, not me.'

Frances sighed. 'Is there a woman in his life, do you think?'

'Bound to be. But no way was I going to ask.'

Leonie went off to begin her search for the dog, but with no real hope of success. Her mood was dark as she drove. What a fool she'd been, she thought bitterly, not to respond wholeheartedly to Jonah in the night. Now it was too late she could see all too clearly that his sole intention had been to make up for his angry, retaliatory onslaught at Brockhill with the kisses and caresses she'd always found so irresistible in the past. And still did. He had never expected her to make love with him in her father's house, with Fenny so close at hand. But like a fool she'd rejected him again, and now she was lucky he even wanted her friendship. Leonie peered into fields as she drove, her eyes steely with resolve. Jonah still responded to her physically, that was obvious. And friendship, even if it *was* only for Fenny's sake, might just warm to other things. If nurtured carefully.

Leonie began the nurturing that very evening, when Jonah arrived. She greeted him sympathetically, asked how he was feeling, warned him not to mention the still absent dog, then took him into the study to join her parents, who were listening to Fenny doing her reading homework. Once Jonah had been provided with a glass of beer, and enquiries made about his well-being, he sat down to join the audience, to Fenny's delight, and afterwards gave her affectionate praise for her prowess, and listened attentively to her account of her day in school.

'I'll take you up, Fen,' Leonie offered, when her mother said it was bedtime.

'Will you come and see me again, Jonah?' asked Fenny as she included him in her round of kisses.

Jonah rubbed noses with her, making her giggle. 'Of course I will, Princess. Goodnight.'

Tom Dysart asked Leonie to tear Kate away from her books to join them. 'Do her good. I have friends who complain their children won't work at all,' he told Jonah, 'but Kate's too much the other way. Rachel was the same.'

When Leonie took Fenny along to say goodnight, she informed Kate she was wanted downstairs.

'Why? What have I done?' said Kate in alarm.

'Nothing. Dad wants you in on a family discussion, that's all.'

'What's a dis—discussion?' asked Fenny, yawning.

'People talking. Boring, really,' said Leonie. 'Come on, sweetheart. One story, then sleep.'

Kate was avidly curious when they went downstairs together. 'Why is Jonah here if it's a family thing? Wait a minute,' she said, beaming suddenly. 'Are you two getting back together?'

'I should be so lucky!' Leonie pulled a face. 'No. It's something quite different, so come on, everyone's waiting.'

Because Kate had been only eleven when Fenny was born, Frances asked Jonah to bear with her while she gave brief details of Rachel's sad love affair. Kate's eyes were bright with tears when Frances had finished.

'I knew Rachel was Fenny's birth mother, of course, but I didn't give much thought to her father, because you said he was dead,' said Kate, sniffing. 'Not that it matters, because Fenny's always been ours anyway, hasn't she?'

'From the very first. But the thing is,' added her father gently, 'in actual fact she's also related to Jonah and his family. Given the choice we'd have informed Jonah's parents at the start, but we gave our sworn promise to Rachel, so that was that.' Tom smiled wryly at Jonah. 'Now Frances tells me you were in on the secret all along.'

Jonah nodded soberly. 'But if Rachel had known what

trouble it would cause she wouldn't have wanted it kept from Leo.'

Leonie smiled at her mystified young sister. 'I broke off our engagement because I thought Fenny was Jonah's daughter.'

'*What?* You're not serious?' Kate stared at her, aghast. 'I may have been only a kid at the time but even I could see Jonah was madly in love with *you*—' She broke off, blushing. 'Sorry.'

'Nothing to be sorry for,' said Leonie, avoiding Jonah's eyes.

'No,' he agreed. 'You're right, Kate. It was my uncle who was in love with Rachel.'

'But he was married to the lady in the wheelchair,' said Kate, frowning.

'Yes,' said Jonah gently. 'My aunt, Helen.'

'But because of my famous temper, the secret is out,' said Leonie, and told Kate about going on the rampage to Brockhill when she'd found Jonah had offered to buy Friars Wood.

'And now,' said Jonah, 'I've come to ask permission to tell my parents.'

'Of course you must,' said Tom without hesitation. 'She's their niece, after all.'

Frances nodded in agreement. 'Poor Rachel. Thank God she never knew the trouble she caused. She was just desperate to avoid hurting Richard's wife.'

Tom Dysart, plainly feeling they'd had enough of emotive subjects for the time being, overruled Jonah's protests and insisted he stay to dinner.

During the meal Frances had a brainwave. 'After you've done some explaining, Jonah, do you think your parents would care to come to lunch on Sunday to meet Fenny?'

'I'm sure they'd be delighted,' he said promptly. 'But it's not the sort of thing to discuss over the phone. I'd better drive up to London tomorrow to see them.'

'Are you fit enough to drive?' asked Leonie quickly.

Jonah smiled ruefully, and touched a hand to his nose. 'Possibly not. If you're going to see Jess, perhaps you'd care to join forces and travel up by train with me, Leo.'

She flushed, shrugging as she met her mother's quizzical eyes. 'I thought a flying visit might be nice since I'm home for a while.'

'Good idea, darling,' said Frances.

'Don't stay too long,' said Kate, rather forlornly. 'Otherwise Fenny'll be upset.'

Leo smiled at her sister reassuringly. 'Just one night and straight back, I promise.'

'If you must travel tomorrow, Jonah,' said her father, 'it might be a good thing to have Leo along for company under the circumstances.'

'I don't feel up to much in the work line for a day or two,' said Jonah frankly. 'So I'll utilise the time off by telling the parents about Fenny and giving a report on Brockhill to my father. He's supposed to be retired, but he likes me to keep him up to speed. Both my parents are interested in the Brockhill property, of course, because they know the area from their visits to Friars Wood when—when Leo and I were engaged.'

'Talking of which, how do they feel about Leo?' asked Frances bluntly, as she handed him the fruit bowl. 'I should keep off the cheese, though, Jonah, if your headache's still plaguing you.'

'Jonah's parents blame *him* for our break-up, not me,' said Leonie ruefully.

'You can put them right at the weekend, then, darling,' said her father, and turned to their bruised, haggard guest. 'You look very tired, Jonah. Let me run you home. Leo can drive your car back tomorrow. Or, better still, stay the night again.'

But Jonah was adamant that he was fit enough to drive such a short distance, and had no intention of trespassing on their hospitality any further. 'And I'll pick you up tomorrow to drive to the station, Leo,' he said firmly. 'Just let me know which train you want to catch.'

Landed with a trip to London she hadn't the slightest desire for, other than the pleasure of seeing Jess, Leo smiled brightly, told Jonah she'd ring him in the morning, but made no attempt to talk to him in private before he went.

'Perhaps you'd better inform Jess you're coming, then,' said Frances, amused, when Tom was watching the news. 'When did you get that idea, Leo?'

'The minute Jonah suggested that friendly terms between us would be more convenient when he came round to see Fenny.' Leonie's eyes flashed. 'So I told him I was off to see Jess. Fool that I am,' she added in disgust.

'Never mind,' said Kate, as she helped clear away. 'Make good use of the train journey together.'

Leonie eyed her challengingly. 'So you think I want Jonah back, do you?'

'Of course you do.' Kate wagged an admonishing finger. 'But you jilted him, remember. It's up to you to make the first move this time round.'

'Out of the mouths of babes—' began Leonie, but Kate shook her head.

'You've been too long in foreign parts, Leo. The word 'babe' means something a bit different these days.'

Leonie raised her hands in laughing surrender, then

went off to ring Jess, and by a miracle found her at
home.

'Stay as long as you like. I'll warn Emily,' said Jess,
yawning. 'Sorry. I've only just got home. I'll try to make
it earlier tomorrow, in honour of your visit. Is there some
special reason? Not that you need one, of course,' she
added, chuckling.

'I'll explain tomorrow,' Leonie promised.

'How about midday?' she asked later, when she rang
Jonah.

'Fine. It gives me time to see one or two people first,
but I've cancelled the rest until next week.'

'How do you feel?'

'I'll live. I was just going to bed. I'll pick you up
around eleven. Goodnight.'

'Goodnight,' she echoed, and put the phone down,
feeling decidedly flat.

Next morning Leonie plumbed new depths of guilt
when Fenny heard about the trip to London.

'Why, Leo?' she wailed. 'Marzi's gone and now
you're going too.'

'I'll be back tomorrow, I promise,' said Leonie, making a vow to curb her impulses in future. 'I'll bring you
back a present.'

'I don't *want* a present, and I don't love you any
more,' sobbed Fenny, and dashed off to the car without
saying goodbye.

'Oh dear,' said Leonie in dismay.

'Don't worry,' said Kate, hoisting her school bag.
'She'll come round. Have a good time.'

'I'll try. See you tomorrow.'

'Fenny gets tantrums, I'm afraid, just like any other
little girl,' said Frances when they were alone. 'She
came rushing downstairs this morning, hoping the dog

had come back, and then heard you were leaving, too. Not a good day for Fenny.'

'I don't have to go, Mother,' said Leonie, feeling worse by the minute.

'Of course you do. Remember what Kate said: use the time to get on better terms with Jonah. If that's what you want, of course.'

Having assured her mother that she wanted it more than anything in the world Leonie almost changed her mind when Jonah arrived. He was neither looking nor feeling his best, it was evident, despite the dark glasses, which hid his bruised eyes, and the strip of plaster across his nose. She took one look at him and held out her hand for his car keys.

'I'll drive.'

'No, you won't!'

Leonie snatched the keys from him, kissed her mother, and ran down the path to Jonah's car, leaving him with no choice but to follow. It was a sunny day, which should have made the drive across the Severn Bridge pleasant, but the atmosphere inside the car had nothing to do with the weather.

'Head bad?' enquired Leonie.

'Nerves, mainly, due to your propensity for the wrong side of the road,' he retorted.

'Look, Jonah,' she said angrily, 'if you'd wanted to travel alone you just had to say. This wasn't my idea.'

'Do you think I don't know that?' he retorted. 'Now for God's sake be quiet and just drive. This stretch of motorway requires concentration.'

Leonie said no more. Other than a brief argument when Jonah insisted on buying their train tickets she maintained a stony silence all through parking the car, and continued it while they waited for the train at Bristol

Parkway. It was obviously too late for mending fences with Jonah. And if he was in this kind of mood much these days maybe she didn't want to bother, anyway.

When they boarded the train Leonie took her place in the first-class seat Jonah had paid for, and picked up the newspaper provided, using it as a shield to avoid looking at him when he slid into the seat opposite.

Jonah plucked it away and stared into her eyes. 'Are you going to stay silent all the way to London?'

'You told me to shut up, so I did,' she retorted, glaring when Jonah began to laugh.

'Pax!' he said, holding up his hands in mock surrender. 'We're attracting attention.'

Leonie cast a hasty glance around, realised he was right and sat back in her seat, face burning. 'I should have stayed at home.'

'But you promised Jess a visit,' he reminded her, grinning.

So he knew she'd lied. With relief Leonie saw a drinks trolley approaching. 'I think I'll have some coffee.'

'It comes free with the ticket during the week.'

'I wouldn't know. I don't usually travel first class.'

'You did last Saturday,' he reminded her.

'The train was full. And at weekends you can travel first for just a few pounds more than the usual fare.'

'Can you really?' Jonah smiled indulgently. 'There, Leo. It isn't so hard to talk to me after all, is it? How would you like your coffee? Black with one sugar?'

She nodded, galled by his patronising tone. But later, when she saw Jonah swallow a couple of pills, she felt remorse. 'Head very bad?'

'It's not wonderful,' he admitted. 'Sorry I yelled at you in the car.'

Leonie smiled a little. 'At least I kept quiet afterwards—which must have done your head *some* good.'

'Not really.' His lips twitched. 'You were so hostile it throbbed even harder.'

Leonie laughed outright. 'I'm not hostile now.'

'And my headache's better already,' he said promptly.

After that the journey progressed more pleasantly. Jonah firmly deserted the personal to outline his plans for Brockhill, assuring Leonie that the modifications to the building would have no adverse effect on other properties in the area.

'As a means of reassuring the local council, I'm using skilled local labour as much as possible,' he went on. 'Getting planning permission was hellish tricky. Your father's support for the project was a great help.'

'Dad was probably glad of some way to make up for your treatment at my hands,' said Leonie soberly, then frowned. 'But why did you want to buy Friars Wood?'

'Oddly enough it wasn't my idea. When the plans were put in front of the board they found that it had once been part of the Brockhill property, and a general decision was made to offer for it. I agreed to ask Tom personally, though I knew he would never accept. Besides, it gave me an excuse to visit your parents. And meet Fenny at last.' Jonah looked at her very directly. 'But when I put the idea to your father I admit the odd thought of revenge did cross my mind where you're concerned, Leo.'

'Especially when you produced that ancient old document to frighten me!'

'I enjoyed that,' he said, his eyes gleaming impenitently. 'Your reaction gave me a very ignoble glow of satisfaction.'

'Did it make up for what I did?'

Jonah's eyes darkened. 'It would take something very different to do that, Leo. But I admit that revenge was sweet.'

'I bet it was,' she agreed ruefully. 'Mind you, I think Dad was sorely tempted to accept your offer. The upkeep of Friars Wood is no joke. But he put the idea of selling up to the vote when we were all gathered together after the party.'

'How did it go down?'

'Like a lead balloon!' Leonie smiled wryly. 'But Mother was dead against the idea, anyway, so the vote was academic.' She explained about her father's qualms over the responsibility Adam was taking on, and exactly what his inheritance would entail. 'Dad had only Rachel to consider, but my baby brother's got three sisters.'

'Four with Fenny,' Jonah reminded her.

Leonie shook her head. 'Rachel left her well provided for, apparently. The rest of us assured Adam we didn't care about the money as long as he kept on Friars Wood, but he suddenly became very grown up and serious, swearing he'd make sure we got our share, whether we wanted it or not.'

'But by that time—far in the future, hopefully—the three of you will be married,' said Jonah without inflection.

'Not necessarily.' Leonie gazed out of the window. 'Jess is in love with her career, and Kate's obviously going to do something high-powered with her flair for sciences.'

'And you?' he prompted.

Leonie shrugged. 'I may still be in my room with a view in Florence.'

Jonah's eyes narrowed, but he made no comment as

the train pulled into Paddington. 'Will Jess be at home now?' he asked, as they made for the taxi rank.

'No. I'm to collect the key from her landlord.'

Jonah helped her into the next taxi in line, gave the driver an unfamiliar address and sat beside her. 'You can go on to Jess later. You may as well come to my place until she finishes work.'

CHAPTER TEN

SECRETLY Leonie considered this a brilliant idea, very much aware that the days were flying by. If she wanted to mend things with Jonah there was no time to lose.

'You could have asked me first,' she said, in token protest.

Jonah shook his head. 'You would have refused.'

'I thought you were going straight to your parents in Hampstead.'

He touched his nose gingerly. 'It seemed best to ring first and warn my mother about this.'

Leonie scrutinised him dispassionately. 'The swelling's gone down. And with the glasses the black eyes aren't noticeable.'

'Good. I've never thought of myself as vain, but I draw the line at giving people nightmares.' He slanted a look at her. 'When you were so hostile in the train the other passengers probably thought I was a battered husband.'

'*I* didn't do the battering!' she retorted, attracting interest from the taxi driver.

'Nor am I your husband,' Jonah whispered in her ear.

Leonie could find nothing to say in answer to that, and lapsed into silence, wondering, not for the first time, how life would have been these past years if their marriage had taken place that summer.

'What are you thinking about?' he asked in an undertone.

'Marriage. How it would have been for us.'

'I doubt it would have been unalloyed bliss, Leo. But it was all I wanted. Back then, at least,' he added deliberately.

Message received, thought Leonie, lashes veiling the light of battle in her eyes. 'When did you move?' she asked, trying for a safer topic.

'As soon as I could after you dumped me.'

Safe topics, it seemed, were in short supply.

Jonah's flat was in a modern, riverside development with a view over the Thames, and familiar from the plans he'd shown her years before, when the complex had been in construction.

'This was your baby, of course,' she said, impressed.

He nodded. 'The only kind available to me now, alas. Lacking the human variety I concentrate on my career instead.'

Leonie kept her temper with effort. 'If you're going to keep twisting the knife, I'll take off to Jess's place right now.'

Jonah gave her a wry, conciliatory smile. 'Meeting up with you again seems to have revived old hurts I thought were healed. I apologise, Leo. Don't go yet, I'd like you to see my home.' When the lift stopped at the top floor he unlocked one of the doors leading off a hushed, carpeted hall, and ushered her inside. 'Welcome to *my* room with a view.'

Bright afternoon sunshine streamed through vast windows Jonah opened onto a balcony overlooking the river. Leonie's first impression was space and light. And emptiness. Every last detail of Jonah's old flat remained vivid in her memory. But in his new home nothing was familiar. A dining table and chairs stood at one end, at the other a pair of big sofas were covered in the natural linen union of the curtains drawn back to display the view. Kilim rugs gave the only note of colour on the polished wood blocks of the floor. There were no ornaments, no fitted carpet, and the white walls were bare.

Leonie looked round, frowning. 'How long have you actually been here?'

'Nearly six years. I had my choice of apartment when the building was finished.' He opened a door into a compact, expensively equipped kitchen. 'Would you like some tea?'

'Thank you.' Leonie perched on a steel and leather stool, watching as Jonah filled a kettle, her heart heavy as she remembered the intimate, domestic tasks they had once shared so joyously. 'Why is the flat so bare, Jonah?' she asked curiously.

He leaned against a counter, arms folded. 'Choice. I like it that way.'

'It's very different from your old place.'

'It was meant to be.' Jonah shrugged. 'Once I accepted the fact that you were gone for good I started erasing all traces of you from my life. I sold some things, sent other stuff to charity shops and threw the rest away. Eventually I was left with nothing to remind me of Leonie Dysart.'

'How you must have hated me,' she said soberly.

Jonah shook his head, his eyes unreadable behind the dark lenses. 'I was filled with hurt, not hate, Leo. Though the purge was amazingly therapeutic. By the time I'd finished I didn't feel any emotion at all. Which was just the way I liked it. I made it clear to all interested parties that I never wanted your name mentioned again, and did my damnedest to cut you out of my life. For years I succeeded quite well. Then the Brockhill property came up and I met your family again, and made Fenny's acquaintance at last. And once I set foot in

Friars Wood there were photographs of you all over the place, and your family talked about you.' He took off the glasses and tossed them onto a counter, his eyes locked with hers. 'I felt as though a block of ice were melting deep inside. And feelings I'd been so sure were dead came alive again no matter how much I tried to suppress them.'

Leonie's heart leapt. 'I could never put you out of *my* mind,' she said huskily. 'I always had Fenny to remind me, looking at me with those eyes of yours—' She broke off, embarrassed to find tears welling up in her own.

Jonah stood tense and still for a moment, then he closed the space between them and took her in his arms, holding her as though she were a piece of Meissen porcelain.

'Will Roberto object if I offer a little tender, loving care?'

'I don't care if he does,' she said recklessly, and buried her face against his shirtfront.

'In that case—' Jonah turned her face up to his and kissed her with the tenderness that had always been an integral part of his lovemaking, like a steady glowing core at the heart of his physical passion.

Leonie's eyes closed, her breath suddenly hurried and her tears dry on her burning cheeks as her lips parted to the tongue which slid between them to caress hers. A tremor of such violent response ran through her entire body she gasped and slid her arms round him, and Jonah's tenderness erupted into fire so suddenly neither of them had any defence against it.

He put her away suddenly. 'Leo, I didn't bring you here to do this,' he said sternly, his eyes like green flames in his tense, bruised face. 'But I want you so much I'm going crazy.'

'So am I,' she said bluntly, gone beyond subterfuge.
'Can't we *do* something about it?'

Jonah seized her in his arms, kissing her with a fe-
rocity she responded to with such ardour he picked her
up and carried her to his bedroom, kicked the door shut,
then put her down on the bed and began to undress her
with feverish haste. 'If you're going to change your mind
do it now!' he commanded at one point.

Leonie shook her head vehemently, but stayed his urgent hands, needing to savour every minute, to make
sure that this was happening, that they were together at
last, in a situation she had dreamed of for so long and
thought would never happen again. She smiled into his
smouldering eyes as she undid his shirt, then bent her
head, her parted lips against his chest as her tongue caressed his skin, and her mouth moved lower in a series
of slow, descending kisses.

Jonah groaned like a man in pain and pushed her flat,
kneeling over her as he stripped off their remaining
clothes. Then slowly, his eyes devouring her, he lowered
himself little by little until they lay together in total contact. Her breath expelled in a relishing sigh as his lean,
naked body settled against hers, and she caressed his taut
shoulders with inciting hands as he kissed her. He moved
his mouth lower to her breasts, to kiss and pull on each
diamond-hard nipple in turn, then at last slid questing
fingers to seek for the sensitive bud at the heart of her
moist arousal, and Leonie gave a choked little cry as
waves of sensation coursed through her body.

At the very point when the exquisite torture threatened
to overwhelm her Jonah's hard muscular thigh nudged
hers apart, and he took possession of her with a long,
sure thrust that pierced her to the core, and she gasped
his name, astonished that this was happening at last for

real, instead of in the dreams that had left her sobbing in the night when she woke alone. Jonah kissed her hungrily as he held her still for a moment, then he began to move, tantalisingly slow at first, but soon with mounting urgency, and she revelled in the fierce, blissful earthiness of it, reassured beyond all possible doubt that this was hot, sensuous reality and she was awake and alive and in seventh heaven. When the inexorable, ultimate pleasure of it overwhelmed her at last they were both half laughing, half sobbing in exultation as Jonah held her fast in the throes of it before surrendering to his own release.

'Dear God,' he gasped against her mouth, his arms still locked around her.

She nodded in mute, breathless agreement.

He raised his head to look at her flushed face, beads of perspiration standing out on his forehead. 'Are you all right, Leo?'

'It depends,' she panted, 'on what you mean by all right.'

His throaty laugh vibrated right through her body. 'I know it's hard to believe, but I brought you here for tea, not this.'

Leonie grinned up at him. 'I'm still waiting for the tea.'

'Do you want some now?'

She thought about it. 'No. Not particularly.' Her eyes widened in sudden remorse. 'Jonah! How do you feel?'

He chuckled. 'Have you got a thesaurus handy?'

'I *meant*,' she said with dignity, 'that your head might be hurting.'

'I don't care a damn if it is. The rest of me feels wonderful.' He rolled onto his side, taking her with him, and held her close, smoothing her dishevelled head against his shoulder. 'You know, darling, I thought this would never happen again.'

She nodded, melting inside at the endearment. 'I used to dream. Of us, together like this. Then I'd wake and remember. And cry.'

Jonah groaned into her hair, his arms tightening. 'What a hellish waste! Years of our lives spent apart for nothing. Why the blazes didn't you stay and confront me that day, Leo?'

'If it had been any other woman I would have come out fighting,' she assured him fiercely. 'But it was Rachel. So all I could do was lie low until the coast was clear, crying my eyes out. Then I rang for a taxi.'

'And vanished out of my life,' said Jonah heavily. He turned her face up to his. 'What now, Leo? Are you going to vanish again?'

Leonie looked deep into the intent, tigerish eyes. 'It depends,' she said at last.

He raised an eyebrow. 'On what, exactly?'

She shrugged, arching her back so that her breasts thrust against his bare chest. 'On what inducement I'm offered to stay. And by whom,' she added, in case he was in doubt.

'What did you have in mind?' he asked, his fingers playing a delicate obbligato down her spine.

Leonie clenched her teeth to control a shiver. 'I'm open to suggestions,' she said unevenly.

Jonah turned on his back and brought her over to lie on top of him. 'My first is to ring Jess, ask if she'd like to have a meal with us somewhere, then apologise because you're spending the night here with me afterwards instead of with her.'

'Am I?' she demanded, smiling down at him.

'Aren't you?'

'Is that what you want?'

'Yes.'

Leonie slid down to lie on her back beside him, and drew the covers over them.

'Cold?' enquired Jonah.

'No. But serious discussion is difficult when— when—'

'Your delectable body is sprawled in total abandon on top of mine,' he finished for her, and turned towards her, propping himself up on one elbow. 'Leo, if this were fiction, I would now reach in some drawer and take out a little box tied with ribbon and hand over your ring.'

'But you threw it away,' she said, resigned, secretly very relieved he was even thinking about rings.

'It was my first reaction,' Jonah admitted. 'But instead of hurling it dramatically into the Thames I sold the ring and gave the proceeds to my mother's favourite charity.' He traced a forefinger across her cheek. 'Do you want another one?'

'Are you offering one?' she demanded. 'If so I want the offer couched with a little more clarity, please—with some romance thrown in.'

Jonah grinned. 'Put your claws in, little lion.'

Her eyes flashed a warning. 'Just you be careful, Jonah Savage. Say what you mean in good plain English or I might get really belligerent—no one would know if I hit you, because your eyes are black already.'

'Kiss me instead,' he cajoled, leaning nearer.

Leonie waited ostentatiously.

'Ah—the magic word,' he said, grinning. '*Please* kiss me, Miss Dysart. After these wounds I've suffered just for you I deserve a kiss.'

'Ah, but will it stop at one?' she said, laughing.

'No.' He kissed her very thoroughly. 'I've been too many years without this,' he muttered against her lips. 'You owe me a great many kisses, my darling.'

'Take them, then,' she said huskily.

Jonah needed no further prompting. When he raised his head at last, he smiled into her heavy eyes. 'Darling, if I kiss you any more the inevitable will happen, and unromantic though it is, alas, my head's beginning to ache again.'

Leonie scrambled up in remorse. 'Let me get you some pills—'

'No.' He pulled her down into his arms again. 'You're all the medicine I want. Let's lie here very quietly for a minute or two—and talk.'

'What about?'

'I need to know certain facts before I proceed.'

Leonie tensed. 'Go on.'

'This Italian—is he expecting to marry you?'

'I think he may be.'

Jonah gave her a slanted, frowning look. 'So he hasn't asked you formally, then?'

'No.'

'And if—when—he does, what will you answer?'

Leonie turned to look him in the eye. 'Until I came home at the weekend I'd fully intended to say yes.'

Jonah sat up, and pulled her up with him, stacking the pillows behind them. 'And now?' he demanded.

Leonie smiled wryly. 'Now I shall say no. Not,' she added swiftly, 'because I'm taking anything for granted where you're concerned, Jonah. Even if I never see you again after today I know I can't marry Roberto.'

'Of course you're not going to marry Roberto,' said Jonah with sudden violence. 'What the hell did you think all that was about just now? Auld lang syne?'

'You tell me!' she retorted.

Jonah slid out of the bed and stalked into the bathroom. He returned wearing a dressing gown, and stood at the foot of the bed, arms folded. 'Pay attention,' he said tightly. 'In the intervening years, Leonie Dysart, I have not been starved of female attention—'

'You mean sex,' she retorted, secretly cut to ribbons at the thought of it.

'All right, sex. What do you expect? I'm normal, single, and women usually like me.'

'You mean lust for you!'

'Will you stop telling me what I mean and listen?' he roared, then winced and clutched his head, glaring at her. 'What I am trying to say is that although there have been women in my life since you left me, none of them has been a permanent arrangement.' He paused, his eyes softening. 'With you it was magic I never found again. Or expected to. So, unlike you, I've never had the slightest desire to marry anyone else.'

'Haven't you?' she said wistfully.

'No. Never,' he assured her.

'Neither have I, really.' Leonie gave him a crooked little smile. 'But I can go one better than you, Jonah. Regarding the sex bit, anyway. I've never made love with anyone else at all. Today was the first time since that last morning with you.'

Jonah stood perfectly still, his eyes narrowed to green slivers of disbelief. 'Not even Roberto?' he asked slowly.

She shook her head. 'I haven't known him long.'

'We hadn't know each other long before *we* first made love,' he reminded her.

'That was different.'

Jonah came to sit on the edge of the bed. 'Why?'

Leonie gazed at him steadily. 'You know why.'

'I always thought I did. Then you left me, and I assumed I'd been wrong.' Jonah took her hand, smiling reminiscently. 'When I kidnapped you out of Rachel's party I wanted to take you home and make love to you there and then.'

'I hoped you would,' she said candidly.

'I wish I'd known that. I spent the entire evening trying to keep my hands off you!' He shook his head. 'I forced myself to hold out for an entire week before doing more than just kissing you goodnight.'

'I thought you didn't fancy me.'

He smiled. 'Darling, you were Rachel's favourite niece, and I was her boss's son. Besides...'

'Besides what?' she demanded.

'I had an idea you weren't nearly as cool and sophisticated as you tried to appear.'

'Oh, did you?'

Jonah took her in his arms. 'It didn't seem possible that no man had ever made love to you, but when I discovered the truth for myself that night—' He breathed in deeply. 'I was overwhelmed in several different ways, not least of them a very primitive sense of possession. From that night on, as far as I was concerned, you were mine and mine alone.'

'I felt the same,' she agreed, and locked her hands behind his neck. 'But try to put yourself in my place, Jonah, and imagine how I felt when I heard you and Rachel that day. If it had been any other woman in the known world I'd have come out and confronted you, believe me.' She rubbed her cheek against his. 'Until that moment you'd been my knight in shining armour.'

'Whereas I'm anything but. Though I admit I abseiled down that blasted cliff to impress you.' Jonah's eyes gleamed with self-mockery. 'And got my just desserts for showing off like a teenager! Unfortunately I'm just an ordinary guy, Leo—'

'Not to me,' she assured him passionately, and reached up to kiss his mouth. 'You're the only man I've ever wanted—ever will want.'

'Until death do us part?' he said very distinctly.

Leonie's eyes lit up. 'At the very least.'

They held each other close for a long time, words no longer necessary. But at last Jonah kissed her hard then pulled her to her feet. 'Let's take a shower, then go shopping for a ring.'

'Yes, please!' Leonie danced ahead of him towards the bathroom, her eyes incandescent with happiness. 'Good thing I brought a change of clothes!' Laughing, she began to gather up the garments Jonah had scattered far and wide.

'Darling!' He caught her hand. 'I thought I'd never hear you laugh like that again.'

Leonie sobered. 'It's years since I did. Oh, Jonah, pinch me, please, and tell me this is really happening.' Jonah laughed and pinched her cheek gently, then turned on the shower and pulled her into the stall with him, insisting he was far too poorly to manage alone. 'I may not be a shining knight, but I did injure myself in your service, Miss Dysart!'

'Let me kiss you better!'

'With the greatest of pleasure.' As she reached up to kiss his mouth he smoothed soapy hands down her back and cupped her bottom, lifting her slightly until she stood on tiptoe, her arms wreathed round his neck to keep her balance, both of them oblivious of the water streaming over them as they held each other close with a simple need for affirmation far removed from the sexual, even held naked in each other's arms.

Later, when they were fully dressed and Leonie's hair was almost dry, she had a bright idea as they left the flat to go shopping.

'I'd rather not go out. Let's buy some food and ask Jess here for a meal instead. She can come round straight from work and I'll make it clear, with sisterly tact, that she's not expected to stay late.' She smiled up at Jonah as they went down in the lift. 'I see no point in wasting precious time in taxis and restaurants.'

'Brilliant idea,' approved Jonah, and gave her a swift kiss before they reached the ground floor. 'Miss Dysart, do you have any idea how much I love you?'

'You can spend a long time telling me after Jess goes home tonight.' Leonie gave him a long, unsmiling look. 'I'll never get tired of hearing you say it.'

'Since you'll have to put up with it for the rest of your natural life that's probably just as well,' he assured her, hailing a taxi.

During the journey Leonie rang Jess to explain the change of plan, but cut off her sister's exclamations by assuring her all would be revealed later. 'Though Jess will jump to the right conclusion, of course,' she said, laughing, then her eyes widened as she realised the taxi was stopping outside the jeweller where Jonah had bought her first ring.

He paid off the driver, then put an arm round her, oblivious of people passing by as he smiled down into her face. 'Call me sentimental, if you like, but I fancied the idea of retracing our steps back to the beginning.'

Leonie blinked hard, afraid to trust her voice.

'But this time I suggest a very different ring,' he said with emphasis. 'Let's forget the other one.'

Leo sniffed, and nodded vigorously. 'Absolutely. I don't mind what the ring's like as long as it fits, so I can wear it right now and never take it off again.'

When Leonie answered the door to Jess that evening she forestalled all explanations by holding out the hand with a band of rubies and diamonds on the appropriate finger.

'Wow!' said Jess, then flung her arms round her sister in a bear hug, grinning up at the man behind her. 'Gosh, Jonah, what does the other chap look like? Did you fight the Italian rival for Leo's hand, or something?'

'Not yet,' said Jonah wryly. 'Do I get a kiss too?'

'Are you sure it won't hurt?'

'Positive,' he said, leering at Leonie in a way which brought such a vivid blush to her face Jess roared with laughter, and gave Jonah a careful kiss on the cheek.

'Nothing more friendly, or big sister will clobber me,' she said, winking outrageously.

'Too true—hands off,' said Leonie, unperturbed. 'Come in and sit down while we do some explaining.'

'What's to explain?' Jess handed Jonah the jacket of her black trouser suit. 'You met Jonah again and realised you were a complete idiot for jilting him and begged him on bended knees to take you back.'

'Not quite,' said Jonah, lips twitching. 'Have some champagne.'

'Champagne!' said Jess blissfully, accepting a glass. She let out a deep sigh as she looked round her at the flat. 'Nice place, Jonah. Have you just moved in?'

'No,' said Leonie, pulling her to sit on one of the sofas. 'He likes it like this.'

'Each to their own, I suppose. Personally, I quite like a cushion or two.' Jess pushed a strand of blonde hair

behind one ear, raising an eyebrow as she looked from
Leonie to Jonah. 'My apologies for my working clothes.'

'It seemed an occasion to wear something special,'
said Leonie, smoothing crushed velvet the exact shade
of her hair. 'I brought this dress to go clubbing with
you, so I thought I might as well wear it tonight. It's not
every day I get engaged.'

'And to the same man,' Jonah reminded her. He
grinned at Jess. 'And not so much of the working
clothes. Even a mere male like me could recognise the
label in your jacket.'

'Probably because you've got the same one in your
own,' she retorted. 'So come on, then, tell all. Well,
almost all,' she added, batting her eyelashes.

'Actually, there's quite a lot to tell, Jess, so make
yourself comfortable,' said Leonie. 'First of all, have
you heard about the dog? That's how Jonah got his
bruises.'

'The *dog*? Explain at once!'

It was still early when Jess insisted it was time for her
to leave. Very serious for once, she kissed Jonah, then
gave her sister a hug.

'I'm very, very happy for you both. That goes without
saying.' She shook her head in wonder. 'But I'm glad I
heard all this from you instead of from Mother during
the weekly call home. It's quite a lot to take in. Poor,
poor Rachel. And poor you, too, Leo. Though how you
could possibly think Jonah was Fenny's father—'

'But you only have to look at her, Jess,' protested
Leonie.

'I don't mean that.' Jess slid her arms into the jacket
Jonah was holding for her. 'I remember how you both
were together, how Jonah so obviously felt about you—'

'And still do,' he said quietly.

'Exactly.' Jess shrugged. 'You must have been mad, Leo, to think he would even look at someone else. In my humble opinion, you should have trusted Jonah, no matter how much the evidence pointed the other way.'

Leonie waited alone in the flat, clearing away the meal while Jonah saw Jess down into her taxi. When he got back she turned to him, stricken, her eyes full of unshed tears.

'Darling, what's wrong?' he demanded, taking her in his arms.

'Jess is right,' she said thickly, leaning against him. 'I should have trusted you.'

Jonah tipped her face up to his and kissed her. 'And I should have come chasing to Florence to demand the truth.' He looked sternly into her eyes. 'But though we did neither of those things we've been given a second chance, Leo, so no more regrets about what might have been. Let's concentrate on what's to come. Which,' he added, in an entirely different tone, 'with regard to the immediate future, was occupying my mind for most of the evening. So come to bed. It's time you thanked me nicely for the ring.'

'You mean it isn't for free?' she said demurely.

'No.' Jonah seized her by the hand and pulled her from the room, pausing in the hall to kiss her. They were both breathing hard when he raised his head. 'I demand your heart—and soul—and body—in exchange, for ever and ever.'

'Amen,' said Leonie fervently.

CHAPTER ELEVEN

LEONIE sat in the taxi next morning in a haze of happiness. Jonah had insisted on coming with her to Paddington, their reluctance to part with each other as strong as their other parting years before.

'It's going to be a long time until tomorrow,' sighed Leonie, as Jonah kissed her goodbye.

'So change your mind and stay. Come with me to Hampstead this morning, and travel back with me tomorrow,' he urged for the umpteenth time.

'You know I would if I could. But I promised Fenny. I must be home in time to fetch her from school.' Leonie kissed him again, then boarded the train before it could go without her. 'Give my love to your parents.'

'I will. Ring me as soon as you get home,' he ordered as the train began to move, giving her a smile of such open possession Leonie kissed her ring in response, and waved her left hand until Jonah was out of sight.

Frances Dysart was waiting at Bristol Parkway when Leonie got off the train, her eyes widening as she took in her daughter's air of dishevelled radiance.

'Had a good time, darling?'

'Wonderful,' said Leonie jubilantly, but waited until she got in the car before she waggled her left hand at her mother.

Frances gazed at the ring incredulously. 'Jonah gave you that?'

Leonie hugged her, laughing. 'I certainly didn't manage to meet someone else in that time, Mother. Besides,'

she added, with a heartfelt sigh, 'there never was anyone
else for me, ever.'

'Oh, darling, I'm so happy for you,' said Frances
thickly, and held her close. 'Has Jonah told his parents?'

'He was on his way to do that after he left me at
Paddington. Then he's coming back tomorrow. He
wanted me to stay tonight—'

'But you'd promised Fenny, of course!'

'Exactly.' Leonie smiled wryly. 'I've managed to exist without Jonah all these years, so I suppose I'll survive
until tomorrow. Somehow. No dog, I suppose?' she
added.

'Afraid not.' Frances heaved a sigh. 'Fenny's pining
badly. I had a terrible struggle to get her off to school
this morning.'

'Poor little poppet. I felt such a heel taking off to
London like that,' said Leonie in remorse, then smiled
at her mother. 'But I'm very glad, now, that I did.'

'So Jonah's forgiven you.'

'Something I'm very grateful for, and jolly well
should be, according to Jess.' Leonie described their evening together, including her sister's parting shot. 'She
thinks I should have trusted Jonah.'

'Jess tends to see everything in black and white,' said
her mother with affection.

'By the way, she's driving down for the lunch party.
Says she wants in on the excitement when Jonah's parents meet Fenny for the first time. Pity Adam's so far
away.'

'We don't know that Flora and James are free yet,'
Frances reminded her.

'Once Jonah tells them about Fenny—and me—I'm
sure they will be,' said Leonie with certainty, then gave
a deep sigh. 'Oh, Mother, I'm so happy.'

When Fenny came out of school that afternoon her woebegone little face lit up when she saw Leonie had come to drive her home. 'You came back!' she said, scrambling into the back seat.

'Of course I did. I promised.'

'I was afraid you'd gone back to that school,' accused Fenny, her eyes on the large parcel beside her. 'What's in there, Leo?'

'Your present. I promised that, too, remember?'

Jonah had bought an outsize Paddington Bear at the station, complete with hat, boots and a suitcase full of the requisite marmalade sandwiches. While they waited for Kate the wrappings were summarily removed, and Leonie's fears that the toy might be too babyish vanished at Fenny's cries of rapture.

'Kate *is* coming home with us this afternoon?' said Leonie suddenly, when they were on the way to the senior school. 'I forgot to ask.'

'Course she is. You promised you'd be home today.' Fenny eyed Leonie with disapproval. 'Kate said we had to share you with Jess, but *she* was sad, too.'

'Oh, darling, I'm sorry! But I'm back now, and when Kate gets here I'll tell you both a secret.'

'Marzi came back?' said Fenny, eyes blazing with hope.

Leonie could have kicked herself. 'No, not yet, darling. But he will. You'll see.'

The moment Kate spotted Leonie she detached herself from a group of friends and raced towards the car, smiling. 'You got back, then,' she said breathlessly, fastening her seat belt. 'Had a good time? Jess OK?'

'Yes, yes and yes,' said Leonie, laughing as she drove off.

'Kate's here now,' prompted Fenny imperiously. 'Tell us the secret, Leo.'

'What secret?' said Kate, then whistled as she spotted the ring on her sister's hand.

'Jonah and I are getting married,' announced Leonie, the words like honey on her tongue.

Fenny let out a squeal of excitement. 'When? Where? Can I be bridesmaid? Alice had a long dress when her sister got married, and satin shoes. Can I—?'

'Hey, steady on,' said Kate, laughing. 'Give Leo a chance, brat.' She smiled at her sister smugly. 'You obviously made good use of the trip, just like I said.'

'It wasn't *quite* like that!'

'I'm sure it wasn't.' Kate was suddenly serious. 'I'm so glad for you, Leo. I bet Mother's over the moon. I think she was afraid you'd never be really happy again.'

'So was I,' admitted Leonie, then chuckled as Fenny drew Kate's attention to her present.

'I *had* noticed,' said Kate, laughing. 'I could hardly miss him.'

'Did you bring Kate a present, too?' demanded Fenny.

'Of course I did—three bestsellers for Miss Bookworm.'

Frances Dysart had a special celebration tea party waiting for them, and once Fenny had recovered from the disappointment of Marzi's absence she ate as many sandwiches and freshly baked scones as the others. During the meal Frances went off to answer the phone, and was away so long Leonie and Kate exchanged questioning glances as they cleared away.

'I wonder who Mother's talking to,' said Leonie.

'Telling Mrs Anderson the glad news, I expect—' Kate broke off as her mother burst into the kitchen, her face wreathed in smiles.

'That was the dog warden! A golden retriever was rescued from the quarry earlier today, and from the description it must be Marzi—'

Fenny let out a scream of joy and hurled herself at her mother. 'Where is he? Let's go and get him *now*—'

'Hey, hey, hold your horses! Let Mother tell us what happened, Fen.' Leonie hauled Fenny on her lap to listen as Frances told them that one of the quarry men had spotted a dog lying on a ledge forty feet down in a disused part of the local limestone quarry. The manager had rung the police, who went immediately to the rescue. The dog was concussed and dazed, with deep scratches on his face and neck, and had been taken to the local vet, who had put him on a drip and was keeping him in overnight.

'What's a drip?' demanded Fenny, alarmed.

Frances explained reassuringly. 'I rang the vet, and he says we can fetch him tomorrow. But here's the best part. Although I'm certain it's Marzi by the description, to make certain the warden said we must watch the local news on television this evening. Would you believe it? A camera crew filmed the rescue!'

After that the excitement was so intense not even Kate could settle to any homework, and Fenny was given a special dispensation to skip hers all together for once.

'Fat chance, anyway,' said Kate, as Fenny danced round the room with Paddington Bear, her face scarlet with joy.

'Ring Dad,' Leonie urged her mother. 'Tell him to get home in time for the news. And we'll video it as well, for Jess and Adam. And Jonah, too,' she added. 'I'll ring him now and give him the glad news.' She jumped up, glad of the excuse, and hurried upstairs to her room to talk in private.

'Guess what?' she said breathlessly, when Jonah answered.

'You've changed your mind!'

'Never,' she assured him huskily. 'Don't even joke about it. Resign yourself to your fate, Jonah Savage. You're stuck with me.'

'Can I have that in writing?'

'I'll hand a sworn affidavit over to you tomorrow. With my love,' she added huskily.

'Talking of which,' said Jonah, his voice deepening. 'Since there's a general celebration at the weekend I demand time alone with you tomorrow night.'

'I've thought of that already. Where shall we go?'

'Just as far as the lodge. Let's have a picnic.'

'Perfect. I'll need to lend a hand here for a while, but after that I'm yours.'

'Damn right you are!'

She sighed with deep satisfaction, then laughed suddenly. 'I'm forgetting—I had a special reason for ringing.'

'To say you love me, of course,' he said smugly.

'That too,' she admitted. 'But the other big story of the day is the return of the prodigal!'

Jonah roared with laughter when he heard about the television coverage. 'You mean I risked life and limb climbing down the wrong cliff?'

'We're not absolutely sure it's Marzi yet—'

'Of course it is. It has to be. How's Fenny?'

'Last seen bopping round the kitchen in transports of delight with Paddington Bear.' Leonie heaved in a deep sigh of thanksgiving. 'Jonah, I wish you were with me right now.'

'Where are you?'

'Sitting on my bed.'

'I'd rather it was *my* bed. Leo, you've got a hell of a lot to make up to me.'

'I'll make a start tomorrow! What time are you coming?'

'I'll ring once I'm on my way, darling.'

'Jonah!' said Leonie in sudden remorse. 'I forgot to ask. How did your parents take the news about Fenny?'

'They were bowled over, as you can imagine. Mother had a little weep at first, but Dad soon cheered her up by talk of shopping for presents.'

'Flora was very sweet to me on the phone. More than I deserve after the way I treated you so badly.'

'She's never quite managed to get her head round that angle,' he said dryly. 'Both of them are utterly delighted we're together again. So am I,' he added, in a tone which made Leonie's pulse quicken.

'I love you so much, Jonah,' she said in a sudden rush, and rang off before she said a whole lot more things better kept until they were together, and alone.

Tom Dysart got home that evening just in time to see the local news, which ended with an item showing the police rescuing a very pathetic, dazed-looking Marzi from the quarry. The dog was last seen looking mournfully through the window of the van bearing him off to the vet.

'A happy ending to a doggy adventure,' said the presenter, and smiled at the camera. 'I'm sure someone out there will be happy to give him a home.'

'He's *got* a home,' yelled everyone in unison, laughing in relief now Marzi had been identified beyond all doubt.

Tom gave Fenny a smacking kiss. 'Right then, Fenella Dysart, no more tears.'

'Dad,' said Kate urgently. 'Haven't you noticed anything?'

Her father eyed her closely. 'In all the excitement, no. Have you had your hair cut?'

'Hopeless!' she said, laughing. 'Show him, Leo.'

Leonie held out her left hand to her father, smiling so radiantly he enveloped her in a bear hug.

'I assume Jonah's responsible for this,' he said gruffly.

'Of course he is.' Leonie grinned up at him. 'I told him he didn't need your permission this time.'

'It's never been withdrawn.' Tom looked at his wife. 'I think this calls for something special to drink with dinner. You were right, Frances—as usual.'

'About what?' demanded Leonie.

Her mother shrugged. 'It was obvious to me since you arrived from Italy that you and Jonah were both still as much in love with each other as ever. Even if neither of you would admit it. The trip to London was a splendid idea. I know they say absence makes the heart grow fonder, but in my opinion a little togetherness is a lot more effective.'

Leonie woke next morning to the feeling of something wonderfully right with her world, and stretched luxuriously as she gazed at the ring on her hand. Sleep had been a long time coming the night before, after a secret midnight call from Jonah to say goodnight. The cellphone was a wonderful invention. She stretched luxuriously as she thought of the outrageously gratifying things Jonah had told her in the quiet night.

The door burst open and Fenny hurtled in, already dressed, with Kate following behind with a mug of tea.

'Special treatment today, Leo,' she said, smiling. 'Hope we didn't wake you.'

'Mummy says it's time to get up soon anyway,' said Fenny. 'You have to go shopping.'

Leonie sat up, accepting the tea with thanks. 'What sort of shopping?' she said, yawning.

'Food, glorious food to celebrate the return of the prodigal.'

'Marzi or me?'

'Both, I should think.'

'Mummy's rung the vet,' broke in Fenny, 'but Marzi can't come home until this afternoon, so you're to wait for me. I want to see him first.'

'Yes, Miss Bossie,' said Leonie, grinning. She waved her sisters off, then slid out of bed, dressed quickly and ran downstairs to eat a hasty breakfast with her mother.

'Mrs Briggs will be here shortly with one of her girls for a blitz on the house,' said Frances, eyeing her shopping list. 'I thought a cold buffet with one or two hot dishes. A spot of informality might be a good thing in the circumstances. But what shall we eat tonight?'

Leonie smiled cajolingly. 'You won't mind if I play truant tonight, Mother? Jonah wants me to have dinner with him.'

Frances looked up, smiling. 'Of course he does. And I don't mind a bit.'

'Great.' Leonie glanced at the clock and jumped to her feet. 'Can we get going, then? I need to be somewhere near home when Jonah rings from the train.'

Frances breathed out a long, heartfelt sigh. 'You were just like this the first time round. I never thought to see it again. You've always seemed a bit detached about Roberto.'

'Roberto!' Leonie's eyes met her mother's in utter consternation. 'Good grief, I'd forgotten all about him.' She jumped up. 'I'll give him a quick ring—'

'A quick *ring*?' Frances looked scandalised. 'You owe the man more than that, Leo.'

'Yes—yes, you're right.' Leonie thrust a hand through her hair. 'I'd better wait until I see him, tell him face to face. Which is something I don't look forward to very much. Not,' she added, 'that there was ever any actual mention of marriage. We never got as far as being lovers, either, in case you're wondering.'

'I'm not. I knew perfectly well you weren't.'

Leonie stared. 'How?'

Her mother looked a little embarrassed. 'Darling, I remember a certain aura about you when you got engaged to Jonah. It's back again, in full force. But you were never like that over Roberto Forli.'

Leonie shook her head in wonder. 'As I've said before, nothing gets past you, Mother dear, does it? But I really must set Roberto straight as soon as I get to Florence.' She pulled a face. 'Only I hate the thought of going back now.'

'When does your contract finish?'

'At the end of next term. Then it's home for the wedding, and this time nothing's going to get in the way!'

Leonie was in the car park of the supermarket, helping her mother load the car, when her phone rang.

'I'm on my way,' said Jonah.

'Good. Where are you?'

'Just leaving London. I'll come straight to Friars Wood.'

'I'll be waiting.'

'Did you sleep well last night?' he said huskily.

'No. Did you?'

'Likewise. Are you alone?'

'No, darling. I'm in a car park with Mother.'

Jonah chuckled. 'And I'm surrounded by men in suits with laptops. See you soon.'

As Leonie banged the car boot shut she gave her mother a cajoling look. 'Could I beg a big, big favour?'

'You want to borrow the car to meet Jonah?'

'Not exactly. Jonah parked his car at Bristol Parkway. Could you possibly drive me over there?' Leonie smiled sheepishly. 'I was going to say I don't think he should drive back by himself, but that's not the reason.'

'You mean you can't wait to see him again,' said Frances, laughing. 'Come on, then. Let's get going. I must get back to help Mrs Briggs.'

Frances made such good time across the Severn Bridge to the station Leonie had a long wait for Jonah's train. She bought some coffee and a magazine, but the time seemed endless until the station announcer said the train was due. She ran up the stairs to cross the bridge to the other platform, watching eagerly as the train came snaking into view. Jonah was first to get off, his dark glasses no disguise for the delight on his face when he saw her. He came striding to take her in his arms and kissed her with a lack of inhibition watched with interest by passengers in the nearest parts of the train.

'What are you doing here?' he demanded, hurrying her towards the stairs.

'Meeting you, of course! Mother gave me a lift over so I could drive you home. I thought you might still have a headache.'

'The only ache I'm suffering from is nothing to do with my head,' he muttered in her ear, then laughed as the colour rose in her face. 'God, I've missed you, Leo.'

'It's only been one night,' she said breathlessly, as he hurried her towards the car.

'It's been thousands of nights, not just one.' He thrust

her into the driving seat, got in the other side and pulled her into his arms to kiss her again. 'Soon,' he muttered against her mouth, 'I'll be able to see you without wanting to do this all the time. But right now I get carnal thoughts every time I set eyes on you. *And* when I don't.'

'Me too,' she admitted frankly. 'You look better, Jonah. How do you feel?'

'I feel wonderful—so do you,' he added huskily, his hands sliding beneath her jacket.

'Mr Savage, would you kindly desist so that I can drive?' she requested, eyes sparkling.

Jonah subsided reluctantly. 'If I must. But I'm glad I'm not driving. I can keep my eyes on you instead of the road.'

On the journey back he reiterated his parents' delight at the news he'd given them, and how much they were looking forward to seeing Leonie and her family again, and their excitement about meeting Fenny.

'Does your mother mind that I'm stealing you away tonight?' added Jonah.

'Not in the least. Once I flashed my ring at her she was ready to agree to anything.'

'Because she's happy about having me for a son-in-law, of course,' he said smugly.

'That, too, conceited one! But mainly because she's happy that I'm happy. And,' she added, slanting a triumphant glance at him, 'while Mother and I were out emptying supermarket shelves for tomorrow's feast I did a little shopping on my own account for that picnic supper you mentioned.'

Jonah sat back in his seat, giving a deep, contented sigh. 'I knew there was more to you than those curls and that luscious pair of—ouch, that hurt,' he complained as she pinched his thigh. 'I was referring to your beautiful dark eyes,' he added, aggrieved, then leered at her outrageously to give the lie to his statement.

At Friars Wood all was in turmoil due to Mrs Briggs and her relentless advance through the house, like Sherman through Georgia.

'Jonah, I'm delighted,' said Frances, kissing him warmly when Leonie took him to the relative calm of the kitchen. 'Though I should warn you that Fenny's determined to be a bridesmaid.'

'Want to change your mind?' teased Leonie.

He looked her in the eye. 'Not a habit of *mine*,' he said pointedly, then put an arm round her waist and kissed her cheek. 'And don't flash those eyes at me. This time I'll make sure *you* don't change your mind, either.'

'I didn't change my mind,' she said soberly.

'No, darling, I know.' Jonah smiled down at her so tenderly Frances turned away hurriedly and filled a kettle.

'Let me get you some lunch—' she began, but Jonah shook his head.

'It's very kind of you, but I really must get back to Brockhill. My father had a few suggestions to make, and I need a word with the architect. And my fax is probably churning out messages as we speak. By the way,' he added, 'wonderful news about the dog.'

'Isn't it just? Fenny's in transports,' said Frances, smiling. 'I'm only sorry you got hurt in vain, Jonah.'

He shook his head. 'Actually, it wasn't in vain. If it took a few bruises to convince Leo that she still cared for me, I'm very grateful to Marzi.'

Leonie suppressed a shiver. 'Speaking of which, take up something less dangerous than climbing as a pastime from now on. Croquet, maybe.'

'Did Leo tell you we taped Marzi's rescue?' asked Frances. 'Spare a minute to watch it before you go.'

Alone in the study, Jonah pulled Leonie on his lap to watch the brief bit of film, amused when Leo described the outcry after the plea for a home for the dog. 'How on earth did he get down on that ledge?'

'Chasing a rabbit, Dad thinks.' She turned to wreath her arms round his neck, kissing him swiftly as the roar of a vacuum cleaner got louder.

'Shall I pick you up tonight?' he asked.

'No. I'll come to you. Are you busy all afternoon?'

'If you want me I'll make sure I'm not.'

'I thought you might like to come to the vet to fetch Marzi when Fenny gets home from school. Are you up to driving?'

'Of course. The only reason I let you drive home was to give my eyes licence to rove.'

'Not only your eyes!' Leonie jumped up. 'Come on, or we'll have Mrs Briggs in here, cleaning round us.'

Later that afternoon Jonah took all four Dysarts down to the surgery to collect Marzi from the vet. The dog staggered out with one of the assistants, still looking dazed, but his tail thumped feebly when he saw Fenny. She gave a cry of dismay and went down on her knees to embrace him, in tears as she saw the bloodstained gouges round his neck.

The young vet, who looked hardly older than Kate, assured Fenny that her dog would soon mend, after a course of antibiotics, and the fur would quickly grow back over his scratches.

'The bump on his head came from the fall, but he probably got scratched by getting caught in a fence somewhere,' she said briskly.

Fenny travelled home in the back of Jonah's car, her

arm round her precious dog. 'I think Marzi should sleep in my room tonight,' she said tremulously.

'He'll be better on his own rug in the scullery, darling,' said her mother. 'He needs to be in familiar surroundings to feel at home again. And you know he's not allowed upstairs.'

'Can I sleep down there with him, then?' demanded Fenny.

The ensuing argument lasted the entire journey. But when they got home Jonah suggested taking Fenny and Marzi for a walk round the garden, and to everyone's relief Fenny was resigned to normal sleeping arrangements by the time they got back to the house.

'Jonah said Marzi might worry if I slept downstairs in the cold,' she announced, frowning in concentration as she struggled to remove the dog's leash without hurting his neck.

'Jonah's right,' said Leonie, giving him a glowing look of gratitude.

'And now I really must get back,' he said with regret. He kissed Leonie swiftly. 'I'll see you later.'

'When?' demanded Fenny.

'After you've gone to bed,' said Leonie firmly, and went to see Jonah out.

'If you love me, get Fenny to bed on time, Leo,' he said, kissing her. 'Quite apart from a normal need to eat tonight, we have things to discuss.'

'What exactly?' she demanded. 'Tell me now.'

'No. I'll tell you tonight. So don't keep me waiting!'

CHAPTER TWELVE

DUE to Frances Dysart's need for help with the meal for next day, Leonie had little time to speculate about the subject of Jonah's discussion. She was forced to keep her burning curiosity in abeyance while she peeled apples, scrubbed tiny potatoes, and concocted a fiery dressing for pasta salad. Kate took on the role of washer-up and cleared up steadily while her mother made bread and pastry and paid constant attention to the ham roasting in the oven. Fenny, demanding to help, was given cheese to grate, and while she laboured talked lovingly to Marzi, who lay in convalescent languor at her feet, occasionally bestirring himself to lick up the odd flake of cheese as it came his way.

Leonie smiled on the hive of industry with deep, inner contentment. Quite apart from her reunion with Jonah, it was so good to be home the thought of leaving grew less attractive by the minute. 'Two parties in such a short space of time is a bit hectic for you, Mother,' she commented.

'I'll lie in a darkened room next week,' said Frances cheerfully.

In the end Tom Dysart had arrived, and Fenny had finished her supper and had been taken to bed before Leonie had a chance to get ready. She rushed through a shower, her hair still damp when she ran to give Fenny a last goodnight kiss before racing downstairs in a hooded scarlet fleece and ancient old jeans.

'Are you going out with Jonah dressed like *that*?' demanded her father.

Leonie grinned, gave a swift explanation, then seized the picnic basket she'd filled, bade a general goodnight and ran out to her mother's car. As she drove into the Brockhill drive the lodge door flew open and Jonah came out, tapping the watch on his wrist.

'You're late,' he accused, taking the basket. 'Come on, Red Riding Hood, I'm hungry.'

'I've been busy, Mr Wolf!' She reached up to kiss him. 'And you'd better keep some of your appetite for tomorrow. Mother's been cooking up a storm.'

'Did I mention food?' He closed the door behind them, dumped the basket on the floor and took her in his arms, smoothing the hood away from her damp hair. 'Leo, your hair's still wet!'

'In my unmaidenly impatience to get here I didn't wait to dry it properly.' She grinned. 'My choice of outfit utterly horrified my father.'

Jonah gave her a comprehensive survey from head to foot, then held her close and kissed her. 'It doesn't horrify me,' he whispered, putting a questing hand to the zip beneath her chin. He slid it open to discover she wore nothing underneath, and stood transfixed in shock for an instant before kissing her so fiercely they were soon panting and breathless, his fingers were drawn like magnets to the nipples which sprang erect to his touch. He tore his mouth from hers at last and yanked up the zip to cover her, his dark-ringed eyes accusing.

'Hell, darling, I'm not Superman. How do you expect me to keep my mind on food when you come dressed like that?'

Leonie scowled. 'I can always go back home—'

'Not on your life,' he growled, and crushed her to

him. 'Tomorrow we'll be surrounded by relations. Tonight you're mine.'

'Only tonight?' she teased, mollified.

Jonah sobered. 'You've been mine from the first moment we met, Leo.'

'I know,' she said, equally grave. 'I've always known it. That's why—'

'Your Italian never had a hope,' he said flatly, and picked up the basket. 'God, Leo, we're so lucky to get a second chance.'

Leonie was deeply aware of it, happiness bubbling inside her as she shared out slices of still warm ham with potato salad, and chunks of her mother's new bread. 'There's only cheese afterwards. You'll have to wait until tomorrow for pudding.'

'I've got all I want right here,' he said, kissing her hand. 'I hope your mother isn't tiring herself out over this. I should have booked a meal somewhere and saved her the trouble.'

'Maybe we could do that some other time. But in the circumstances, with Fenny and so on, it's best we're at home.' Leonie gave him a challenging look. 'Right, Jonah, I've been patient long enough. What was so important that it had to wait until now to discuss?'

'Let's finish supper first.' He smiled at her. 'Don't look like that, darling. Nothing's going to come between us again, I promise, no matter what happens. I forgot the wine,' he added suddenly, and made to get up, but she pulled him back.

'Just as well. I'm high on adrenaline anyway, and just a bit tired. A glass of wine would probably have me on my back in no time—' She blushed at the look in his eyes. 'Don't say it,' she said fiercely.

'Say what?' He smiled innocently, and cleared his plate with a sigh of satisfaction. 'That was perfect.'

'Come *on*, Jonah,' she urged. 'Talk. Or I'll expire with curiosity.'

He dumped their plates on the floor and drew her close. 'This is a bit difficult—'

'Why?' Leonie eyed him suspiciously. 'Is it to do with a woman?'

'Yes,' he said promptly, grinning as she bristled. 'And don't even think of hitting me in my present state. Besides, the woman is you, Leo.'

'Oh.' She subsided uneasily. 'Go on, then.'

'In the past,' he began, 'I always took care to make sure you didn't get pregnant by accident.'

'I know.' A shudder ran through her. 'That's why I was so shattered about Rachel.'

Jonah pulled her closer, smoothing her head against his shoulder. 'Leo, I really did take you to my place for tea when we got to London the other day. I honestly never anticipated what actually happened. And when it did the thought of precautions never entered my head. Not until later, anyway. And from your startling, wonderful revelation about your own love-life I doubt that you were doing anything about birth control either.'

'Of course I wasn't,' said Leonie serenely.

Jonah frowned, and tipped her face up to his. 'You're remarkably laid back about this.'

She shrugged. 'As you say, by the time I had any thought to spare for such things it was too late, anyway.'

'And you don't mind?'

'The risk of a baby?' Leonie shook her head. 'As long as it's your baby, Jonah, no.'

'Thank God,' he breathed, and kissed her fiercely. 'If

I'm honest, I think it was a pretty Freudian lapse. A way to be sure we'd get married this time.'

'For me too,' she admitted. 'But I was already sure, Jonah. The real moment of truth hit me when I thought I'd lost you down that cliff. From then on it was time for desperate measures to get you back. So I decided to seduce you any way I could.'

Jonah's eyes smouldered. 'I wish I'd given you the chance to try!'

'A good thing you didn't. I've never tried to seduce anyone, so I'd probably have botched the whole thing!'

He laughed indulgently. 'Leo, your success was assured, believe me. Surely that was obvious when we danced together at Adam's party? I could have thrown you on the floor and made love to you there and then.'

'Then why were you so horrible when I came here the following night?' she demanded, eyes kindling.

'I was hopping mad, Miss Dysart.' Jonah tapped her cheek with an admonishing forefinger. 'When you came storming in here, throwing wild accusations at me, I lost my temper, and retaliated in the way I knew you'd resent most of all.' His eyes gleamed. 'Besides, I needed to know if you still responded to me.'

'And I did,' she said in disgust. 'Right here on this sofa. Did you enjoy your revenge?'

'In a way. But it backfired, because in the end I was more aroused than you were. I'll never know how I managed to break away.' His eyes darkened at the thought of it, making her heart beat faster.

'You don't have to break away now,' she said unevenly, but he shook his head.

'Not yet. There's something I want you to do for me.'

'Anything in the world,' she promised recklessly.

'I hope you mean that, Leo, because quite apart

from the possibility of a child, I don't want to let you out of my sight for long again.' He took her face in his hands. 'Don't go back to Florence, darling.'

'I'm not going to.' She laughed in delight at his astonishment. 'I'll get in touch with the principal and ask him to get a substitute teacher for the summer term—'

Jonah crushed her mouth under his, his arms threatening to crack her ribs, but, suddenly impatient, Leonie pushed him away and stood up, unzipping the fleece and tossing it away.

'I thought you said this was a sofabed,' she said huskily, standing with her hands clasped behind her back.

Jonah got up very slowly, his eyes riveted on her. Suddenly he came to life, tearing off his shirt as he leapt to seize her in his arms, his hands flat against her back to hold her against his bare chest.

'It seemed a shade lacking in subtlety to have a bed ready and waiting,' he said hoarsely, and slid his hands round to cup her breasts, his thumbs brushing the tips into sensitive, erectile conductors which set up a chain reaction of wanton heat streaking through her entire body.

'Jonah,' she gasped, her hand sliding over the taut musculature of his shoulders. 'Let's make sure. Let's make a baby. Right now.'

They gazed into each other's eyes, breathing hard, then Jonah's lit with sudden, defusing laughter. 'If you mean that give me time to do something about this sofa. I refuse to conceive my first-born on the floor.'

They unfolded it together in desperate, clumsy haste, but once it was ready they were content just to lie holding each other for a while.

'This is how it should be,' said Leonie, rubbing her cheek against his shoulder.

Jonah chuckled. 'In a makeshift bed, in a cold, half-empty cottage?'

'No!' She nipped his skin playfully. 'I meant that in your flat the other day it was like a bolt from the blue, an irresistible force that swept us away. I had no more thought about consequences than you did.'

'I'm glad I wasn't the only sinner,' he said wryly, and turned her face up to his. 'But we made love again that night, remember. I'd had plenty of time to think by that time.'

'So had I,' she pointed out. 'Did I voice any objections?'

'No. And by then you were wearing my ring.' Jonah smiled reminiscently. 'It was all you *were* wearing.'

'Just like now!' Leonie stretched luxuriously against his responsive body. 'But I'm serious, Jonah. This time it ought to be different.'

Jonah shifted so that they lay facing, looking into each other's eyes. 'You mean you want a love-child, not a happy accident.'

'Exactly!' Leonie smiled with passionate gratitude. 'You always could read my mind.'

'Can you read mine now?' he asked, pulling her closer, his body hard and ready against her.

She laughed breathlessly. 'I don't need to!'

Jonah began to kiss her with a slow, savouring relish she responded to with such ardour the speed of their loving quickly accelerated. Mutual heat flamed higher as his mouth moved lower, his hands cupping her breasts to receive his seeking lips, resulting in such delicious torture she retaliated with caresses of her own. But Jonah stayed her hand, flipped her on her face and held her still while he kissed every inch of her from the nape of her neck to her heels. At last he turned her back again, his eyes holding hers as his fingers slid slowly upwards from ankle to knee and higher, until she was at breaking point by the time he reached his goal, his caresses causing such hot turbulence it affected them both in equal measure. Controlling himself with superhuman effort, Jonah took time to press a kiss to each bare knee before he thrust himself home between her thighs with a sureness Leonie greeted with a gasp of deep, visceral pleasure, arms and legs around him in passionate embrace as they surged together in perfect, accelerating rhythm to achieve their hearts' desire.

CHAPTER THIRTEEN

IT WAS very late by the time Leonie got to bed. Jonah had been adamant about going back to Friars Wood in the car with her, preferring a walk back to Brockhill to the alternative of seeing her drive off there alone in the middle of the night. After a lengthy farewell she had let herself in by the back door as quietly as she could, grateful that Marzi was still in too dazed a state to make much fuss at the sight of her.

Leonie had set her alarm before getting into bed, afraid she might sleep late in the morning, but though she fell asleep quickly enough she was awake long before her clock roused her. She lay gazing out at the bright morning, and smoothed a gentle hand over her midriff, wondering if her night of love with Jonah had produced the longed for result. She slid out of bed, suddenly too full of energy to stay there any longer, and went off to have a bath. And discovered red marks here and there on her skin in interesting places, her face equally red as she remembered how she'd acquired them.

Early as it was, the kitchen was already filled with the scent of roasting meat, and Frances Dysart looked up from her breakfast in surprise when Leonie joined her. 'Good morning, darling, you're early.'

'It seemed like a good idea today.' Leonie bent to fondle Marzi, who'd come to greet her with something of his old exuberance. 'Hello, old boy. You're looking a *lot* better.' She smiled at her mother. 'I thought I'd be early enough to take Marzi out for you. Fenny and Kate are still asleep.'

'I've already taken him for a quick run round the garden. Your father can give him a longer walk later, with Fenny.' Frances poured tea for them, smiling at her radiant daughter. 'You obviously had a lovely evening with Jonah.'

'I certainly did. I'm afraid it was late by the time I got home.'

'I know. I heard you come in.'

'Sorry! I tried to be quiet.'

'I wasn't asleep. Not,' added Frances hastily, 'that I consciously stayed awake.' She smiled sheepishly. 'I couldn't help wondering about the kind of wedding you want.'

'As long as it's as soon as possible, I don't mind,' said Leonie promptly, reflecting that 'soon' was a good idea in more ways than one if her instincts were right. She looked up to find her mother regarding her with amused resignation. 'Sorry. Did you say something?'

'Yes, darling. Several times. But never mind. We'd better get today over first, before we start talking about weddings. What time are Flora and James arriving?'

'I told Jonah to say one-ish, to give Jess time to get here. But Jonah's coming down from Brockhill fairly early. I thought he might come in useful.'

'And you just want him here anyway,' teased her mother.

Leonie roused Fenny and helped her dress, and kept her away from Marzi long enough to eat some breakfast, then asked her mother for a list of tasks, and had finished most of them by the time she made her phone calls to Italy. There was no response from Roberto's number, but Leonie got through at once to the Ravellos. Her news was received with much regret, but also with welcome sympathy, since Angela, the British wife of Luigi Ravello, the principal, had witnessed first hand Leonie's anguish after breaking up with Jonah. The school, she informed Leonie, would not open until well after Easter anyway, and if another teacher was impossible to acquire in the time she would reorganise the timetable and take on some of Leonie's lessons herself.

Leonie was jubilant when she opened the door to Jonah later. He dumped down a bag of clanking bottles, and hugged her tightly when she gave him the glad news.

'I think my willingness to work long hours over the years stood me in good stead,' she said happily, reaching up to kiss him.

'Wonderful,' said Jonah fervently. 'Not that it matters. I wouldn't have let you go back, anyway.'

'You're very masterful this morning,' she teased.

'I was masterful last night, too,' he reminded her softly. 'Did you sleep well?'

'Very well. How do *you* feel this morning?'

'I feel good. And if appearances are anything to go by, you feel the same way.'

'I do,' she assured him, then laughed as Fenny came running along the hall.

'Jonah,' she said urgently. 'Can I be your bridesmaid?'

'Oh, definitely,' he said promptly. 'How about Kate and Jess?'

Fenny nodded happily. 'And Marzi, too. He can wear flowers round his neck.'

Jess surprised everyone by arriving early, wearing huge dark glasses and a linen trouser suit a shade or two darker than her hair. 'Am I in time for all the fun?' she demanded, running up the steps in stilt-heeled backless sandals.

'How on earth do you walk in those?' asked Kate enviously.

'I don't, cupcake, I take taxis!' Jess gave her sisters an affectionate squeeze. 'Great news about the dog,' she said, grinning. 'Between you and Marzi, Leo, the family must be in a state of constant euphoria.'

'How about you?' said Leo in an undertone, as they followed Kate to join the others. 'How's the new man?'

'History.' Jess shrugged philosophically. 'Not my type after all. Never mind, some day my prince will come, I suppose.'

'When he does, make sure you hang on to him,' advised Leonie. 'I took your little homily about trust to heart, by the way.'

'Wise move. Men like Jonah are few and far between. Come on—I need that coffee!'

The meal was ready, it was a few minutes before the arrival of the guests, and the family was gathered for a pre-lunch drink in the drawing room when Jess came hurrying in to say she'd answered the phone on her way downstairs.

'Jonah, don't say your parents can't come after all,' said Frances, jumping up, but Jess waved her back.

'It's for Leo, not you, Mother. A man with the sexiest voice in the known world is asking for her.' She grinned wickedly at Jonah. 'Says his name's Roberto Forli.'

Cursing herself for leaving a message on Roberto's machine, Leonie bent to give Jonah a very deliberate kiss, then went off to the hall to pick up the phone.

'*Ciao*, Roberto, that was quick,' she said brightly.

'Quick? You joke with me, Leonie. It is days since I spoke to you last. I tried to ring last night, but your phone does not answer. So today I asked the hotel receptionist to find out the number of your parents' house, and, *allora*, I am speaking to you at last.'

'Roberto, I'm so sorry,' she said guiltily. 'Things have been very hectic here.'

'Leonie, I also am here,' he announced in triumph. *'Here?'*

'In your town of Pennington, *tesoro*,' he said, laughing. 'I told you I would surprise you.'

Leonie sagged against the wall. 'You've certainly done that.'

'I booked a room at this hotel because naturally I would not intrude on your parents before meeting them formally.'

For which she was deeply thankful. 'Look, Roberto, we're in the middle of a family party right now, so I can't get away. But I'll come and see you this evening.'

'But of course. I have already booked dinner here at the Chesterton, Leonie. Would your parents care to join us? I am most anxious to meet them.'

'Not tonight,' she said swiftly.

'Ah. You want me to yourself,' he said with satisfaction.

'Actually, Roberto, I have something to—to discuss with you.'

'Then I shall wait with impatience to listen, *carissima*.'

'I'll be there about seven-thirty,' she promised, and put the phone down to see Jonah standing in the doorway, eyes slitted in his set face.

'You'll be where at seven-thirty?' he demanded.

'Roberto's at the Chesterton in Pennington. He's flown over to see me—'

'And just when was all this arranged?'

'It wasn't. It's Roberto's idea of a surprise. He tried to ring last night but I switched off my phone before I came to you.' Leonie looked him in the eye. 'I knew nothing about it, Jonah, but now Roberto *is* here it's the perfect opportunity to speak to him in person.'

'Is it really?'

'Yes.' Her chin lifted defiantly. 'You don't want me to go back to Florence, remember, so it's only fair that I tell Roberto, face to face, that I'm going to stay here and marry you.'

'I'll come with you,' said Jonah grimly. 'Just in case he needs convincing.'

'You will *not*,' she retorted.

'Hell, Leo, after last night do you expect me to look on meekly while you waltz off to see your former lover?' He seized her by the shoulders, shaking her slightly.

'He never was my lover!'

'Whatever he is, I refuse to let you go on your own,' he snarled, dropping his hands.

'Go where?' enquired Jess, coming to join them.

Jonah turned to her in appeal. 'Leo's off to see this man Forli tonight, and actually expects me to be magnanimous about it.'

'What's so odd about that?' demanded Leonie. 'Roberto's a good friend—'

'Friend!' said Jonah scornfully.

'Yes, friend!'

'Then if he's such a good friend he won't mind if I tag along, will he?'

They stood glaring, eye to eye, like boxers before a fight.

Jess sighed impatiently, and stepped between them like a referee. 'Pack it in, you two, or you'll spoil the day for everyone.'

Jonah backed down a little. 'Just ring the man and explain on the phone, Leo.'

'I can't do that,' she said in despair. 'I know what it's like to be hurt—'

'So does Jonah,' her sister reminded her.

'Thank you, Jess,' he said, with an ironic bow.

'Don't thank me. None of my business.' She brushed back a strand of bright hair. 'If we weren't expecting guests I'd leave you both to it. But my mother's worked hard to prepare for this party, so kiss and make up, OK?'

But Leonie wasn't even listening. She was staring through the window, her eyes on the car drawn up on the terrace. *'Jonah!'* she said in alarm.

He put an arm round her at once. 'What is it, darling—? Good God!'

'Wow,' said Jess, peering over her sister's shoulder. 'Did you know about this, Jonah?'

'No, I didn't,' he assured her.

'I'll run and fetch the others,' said Jess, and raced off as fast as her heels would allow.

'I'd better give Dad a hand,' said Jonah, pulling himself together, and took Leonie by the hand as they went outside to hurry down to his father's car.

Helen Savage smiled uncertainly from the back seat. 'I'm gatecrashing, I'm afraid, Leonie. Flora insisted on bringing me. She persuaded me you wouldn't mind.'

CHAPTER FOURTEEN

LEONIE recovered herself swiftly. 'Of *course* we don't mind. How lovely to see you!' She leaned through the window to give the thin, fragile cheek a welcoming kiss, then turned to smile at James Savage as he got out of the car. 'It's so good to see you again, too.'

Jonah's father was an older, greyer, slightly less tall version of his son. He gave Leonie a swift hug. 'Welcome back, my dear. Wonderful news. We couldn't be more pleased—but excuse me for a second, we need to extract Helen's chair.'

Flora Savage rushed to embrace Leonie affectionately, then smiled reassuringly at her sister-in-law as Jonah lifted her out of the car. 'Don't look so worried, Helen. The Dysarts are very hospitable people. Frances will take an extra guest in her stride, won't she, Leo dear?'

'Of course she will,' said Leonie promptly.

Flora took her hand and squeezed it reassuringly. 'Don't panic. Helen is as eager to meet Fenny as we are.'

Leonie smiled in radiant relief as Jonah carefully deposited his aunt in the wheelchair James Savage had set up in the porch, wishing she had time to warn her parents. But when they came hurrying to greet their guests, neither of them displayed anything but the warmest of welcomes when they found Jonah's parents had brought Helen Savage with them. There was a general round of greetings, then the guests were ushered into the house, and pressed to a celebratory glass of champagne to mark the occasion.

'Where's Fenny, Jess?' whispered Jonah, as his father wheeled Helen towards the drawing room.

'Kate's washing her face and hands. She'll bring her down in a minute.' Jess blew out her cheeks. 'Silly, I know, but I feel nervous.'

'Me too,' agreed Leonie.

Once they were settled in the drawing room everyone was soon so engrossed in general wedding talk Helen Savage visibly relaxed in the sincere warmth of her welcome. Then Leonie saw her tense as Kate led in a tidy, unusually shy Fenny. Confronted with three strangers, one of them in a wheelchair, Fenny's usual exuberance was missing. Jonah crossed the room, smiling, to take the new arrivals by the hand.

'The remaining Dysart ladies,' he announced, steering them across the room. 'You've met Miss Katharine before, of course—take a bow, Kate. And this is Fenella.'

'Come on, Fenny,' said Frances lovingly. 'Don't be shy. This is Jonah's mummy and daddy, and this lovely lady in the special chair is Jonah's aunt.'

Leonie held her breath as she watched Helen Savage gaze, mesmerised, into the elfin face of her husband's daughter.

'Hello, Fenny,' said Helen at last, and smiled into the unmistakable eyes. 'I hear your dog had an amazing adventure this week. I'd love to hear all about it.'

Fenny beamed, all shyness gone at once. 'His name's Marzi. He's in the kitchen because Mummy won't let him come in here. He was naughty and ran away, and Jonah climbed down the cliff to look for him and hurt his face. But Marzi was in the quarry all the time.'

From that moment on the occasion was a foregone

success, with everyone in party mood as they toasted the engaged pair and enjoyed Frances Dysart's excellent meal. Leonie kept a watchful eye on Helen Savage from time to time, but it soon became plain that Helen was enjoying herself enormously, and making no secret of the fact that she couldn't keep her eyes off Fenny.

Fenny had a quite wonderful time, particularly when she discovered that Jonah's mummy had brought presents for everyone, including a doll and several sets of clothes for herself, and even a leather bone for Marzi. She settled herself on the carpet to change the doll's clothes, delighting Helen by asking for help when she couldn't manage the tiny buttons and fasteners.

'I hadn't a clue about this,' said Jonah in the kitchen later, watching Leonie make coffee. 'My mother's idea, needless to say. Dad said she felt Helen had a right to know about Fenny, and Mother was right, of course.'

'Did Helen know about Rachel?' asked Leonie.

Jonah looked at her thoughtfully. 'I'm not sure, but I'm beginning to think she did. If she couldn't share the physical side of marriage with Richard, maybe she preferred the idea of his relationship with Rachel to the obvious alternative.'

'I suppose Fenny ought to know the truth at some stage.' Leonie pulled a face. 'Not that I want to be the one to tell her!'

'Leave the decision to your parents.' Jonah caught her hand and turned her towards him. 'Changing the subject, Leo, are you still going to Pennington tonight?'

'Yes, I am. I *must*, Jonah. Please try to understand.' She looked down at the hand he was crushing. 'If I do, will you want this ring back?'

'Of course not!' he said scornfully. 'What I want, Leonie, is for you to see my point of view. Why the hell do you have to *meet* Forli to break the news to him? Just ring his room at the Chesterton and tell him what's happened. Surely the man's civilised enough to understand.'

'Of course Roberto's civilised, and he probably will understand. But he's also a good friend and I'm fond of him,' she said stubbornly. 'After coming all this way to see me he deserves more than a phone call!'

'I fail to see why. You didn't ask him to come. Did you?' he added suddenly.

'No, I did not. Why are you so dead against my seeing him? Don't you trust me?' snapped Leonie, glaring at him.

'Where's the coffee?' demanded Kate, joining them. 'Mother's getting fidgety in there.'

'Sorry,' said Jonah swiftly. 'My fault, Kate. I've kept Leo talking.' He picked up the tray and strode from the room.

'Oops!' Kate pulled a face. 'I obviously hit on a bad moment.'

Leonie shrugged philosophically. 'Just as well you did. You take the chocolates in, love, I'll be along in a minute. I need a minute or two with a lipstick.'

When she rejoined the party Jonah was sitting on the floor with Fenny, helping her with one of the complicated puzzles his mother had brought her. He looked up at her approach, but made no indication that he wanted her to join them. In response to Flora Savage's beckoning hand Leonie went to sit beside her instead, the strain of playing the role of happy bride-to-be so intense she was thankful when James Savage said it was time to leave.

'Flora's taking Helen back to the flat in Pennington for the night, to save a tiring drive back to London,' he told his son. 'But if you can tear yourself away, Jonah, I'd be glad of a walk round Brockhill for a while, to visualise some of the modifications for myself. You can give me a lift into Pennington later, if you would.'

Afterwards, during the general kissing and leavetaking, Jonah took Leonie by the shoulders and looked into her eyes for a long, questioning moment before giving her a swift peck on the lips—purely, she knew, because it was expected of him. She felt cold inside as his parents embraced her and reiterated how happy they were, and when the two cars drove off Leonie joined the rest of her family to wave them out of sight. Indoors there was general agreement that the lunch party had been a great success.

'Though I was secretly shattered when I saw Helen Savage,' said Frances with feeling. 'But Flora told me later that she felt Helen had a right to—to meet us all again,' she added, with a look in Fenny's direction.

'Come on, Fen,' said Kate quickly. 'I'll get out of the washing up if we take Marzi for a walk.'

'Skiver!' said Jess, taking off her jacket. 'Right, then. I got off scot-free last time, so it's my turn today.'

'You look exhausted, Mother,' said Leonie. 'Go and lie on a sofa with a book. I'll help Jess.'

'Any instructions for me?' said Tom Dysart indulgently.

'Go up for a nap,' said Jess, and smiled at him cheekily. 'Weren't you going to do that anyway?'

He nodded, yawning. 'But it's nice to be given permission!'

When Leonie and Jess had banished everyone from the kitchen, they worked quickly and efficiently together.

'Did I detect a certain frost when Jonah went?' asked Jess.

'You did.'

'Same subject?'

'Yes.' Leonie's mouth set stubbornly.

'So you're determined to see your Roberto tonight, then?'

'He's not *my* Roberto, which is the whole point of the exercise, Jess. I need to tell him that. And tell him about Jonah at the same time. If the wedding's still on,' she added with gloom.

'Surely Jonah didn't deliver an ultimatum!'

'As good as.'

Jess stacked plates on a tray with concentration, frowning thoughtfully. 'Not into a spot of retaliation by any chance, is he?'

'He's not above such things,' agreed Leonie, 'but in this case it goes deeper than that.'

'Maybe he doesn't fancy some chum in Pennington spotting his bride-to-be out on the town with a handsome Italian—I assume Roberto *is* handsome?'

'I suppose so.' Leonie's eyes narrowed. 'But I don't think it's that, either. Maybe Jonah feels I owe it to him to do as he asks. To make up for what happened before.'

'Quite possibly.' Jess went on drying glasses for a moment, then snapped her fingers in inspiration. 'I've got an idea. A solution of a kind. Roberto won't like it, but Jonah will.'

Leonie eyed her sister narrowly. 'Are you volunteering to dine with Roberto instead of me, by any chance?'

'No way,' said Jess, smiling like a Cheshire cat. 'But I'll tag along *with* you. A nice dinner at the Chesterton is rather appealing. Do you think Roberto will feed me as well?'

Leonie grinned. 'I'm sure he will. That's a *brilliant* idea, Jess. I'll ring Jonah and tell him—' She halted.

'No, I won't. You were the one talking about trust, Jess. This time Jonah should be trusting me. I won't embarrass you with the details, but he has good reason to, believe me.'

Leonie had expected to hear from Jonah every minute while she was getting ready later, but the only phone call came from Flora Savage, to say how much they'd enjoyed the party and how grateful Helen had been to meet Fenny.

'Poor Rachel had no need to keep her existence secret after all,' said Flora sadly. 'Helen is a very special person, Leo, dear. She's glad Rachel gave Richard a child.'

Leonie was very quiet on the journey to Pennington, happy to let her sister drive.

'No word from Jonah, then?' asked Jess, before they set out.

'No.' Leonie looked down at the ring on her finger. 'But I'm not giving this up—and everything it stands for—without a fight.'

If Roberto Forli was taken aback to find Leonie had brought her sister along, he concealed it with admirable aplomb. As he came down the stairs to the foyer of the Chesterton, Jess exchanged a speaking glance with Leonie. He was wearing a pale, unstructured suit, of the type that needs a muscular body to carry it off, and moved with the co-ordinated grace of the champion skier. His heavy-lidded oval eyes were dark and his nose imperious in a tanned face framed in close-curling hair of the dark blond shade common in Northern Italy.

'Leonie!' he said, smiling, and kissed her on both cheeks before turning to Jess. 'And who is your beautiful companion?'

'My sister Jessamy,' said Leonie. 'Jess, may I present Roberto Forli?'

'*Piacere!*' said Roberto, bowing over Jess's hand.

'How do you do?' she responded, smiling. 'Are you here for long, Signor Forli?'

'Roberto, please,' he entreated, and cast a glance at Leonie. 'I return to Florence in the morning. Come,' he added, 'we shall sit in the bar with a glass of wine while we choose the meal.'

Leonie had instructed Jess to wait until the meal was over before leaving her alone with Roberto. She would have preferred to say her piece straight away, but couldn't bring herself to spoil the entire evening for Roberto, who, with innate grace, was asking Jess animated questions about her life in London, as though her presence added the crowning touch to the evening instead of depriving him of time alone with Leonie.

Roberto asked about the birthday party, and they both described it to him in every detail bar one, and then Leonie told him about the dog's adventures, which amused him enormously. During the meal Leonie could see that Jess was very taken with Roberto Forli, whose manners were impeccable, despite the questioning look he sent in Leonie's direction from time to time.

'Right,' said Jess briskly, once coffee was served. 'If you'll excuse me I must make some phone calls, so I'll leave you two to chat for a while. Thank you for the meal, Roberto.'

'*Prego,*' he said, jumping up to hold her chair. 'But please do not feel you must absent yourself.'

'It's very kind of you, Roberto, but nevertheless I will,' she said firmly, smiling up at him as he held her jacket for her. 'I'll be in the bar later, Leo.'

Alone with Roberto, Leonie decided to set matters in

motion by taking her ring from her handbag to slide it on her finger. 'I'm going to marry someone else, Roberto,' she said quietly, holding out her hand.

Roberto stared at the ring in stunned silence, then brought his dark eyes up to meet hers, his face suddenly stern. 'So. I knew, when you brought your beautiful sister with you, that something was wrong, Leonie. But could you not have warned me? And how has this happened so quickly?' He smiled in self-derision. 'I have been so careful to court you with patience, to control my natural instincts and wait until your feelings were as warm as mine. *Stupido!* It is obvious, now, that I would have waited for ever!' His eyes narrowed. 'I would very much like to meet this man who took you by storm.'

Heaven forbid, thought Leonie, suppressing a shudder. 'I was engaged to him before. Years ago. Long before I met you. When we met again I realised I'd never stopped loving him.'

Roberto flinched. 'You have made a fool of me, Leonie,' he said harshly.

'It was never my intention!'

He made a dismissive gesture. 'I should have contacted you before I left Firenze.' He gave a mirthless laugh. 'But, like a fool, I wished to surprise you.'

'You succeeded,' she said miserably. 'I'm so sorry, Roberto. I could have rung you, I know, but it seemed so cold and unfeeling to tell you over the phone.'

'You were wrong. I would have preferred that to *this*,' he retorted. 'You have taught me a lesson, Leonie. I shall never give in to impulse again.' He rose to his feet and came round to hold her chair, coldly punctilious. 'And now we must rejoin your tactful sister. Do not misunderstand me, Leonie, it was a pleasure to meet her, but you had no need for protection. Were you afraid to face me alone?'

'Certainly not,' she said, stung. 'But Jonah—my fiancé—strongly objected to my coming here alone tonight. When I refused to explain things to you via a phone call he wanted to come with me. I thought it best to spare you that, so I brought Jess instead.'

'I understand his objection very well,' said Roberto coldly, as they walked back to the bar. 'It is a natural one for any man.'

They found Jess in a corner of the crowded bar, receiving a tray of coffee from a waiter. When she saw them she got up quickly. 'Time to go?' she asked, looking from one face to the other.

'Yes,' said Leonie and glanced up at her hostile companion. 'I've had my say, and made my apologies. I'd like to go home now.'

'Do you mind going on out to the car?' said Jess, 'Just give me five minutes' grace. If I'm driving I must have some of this coffee before I start.'

'But of course,' said Roberto politely. 'I shall escort Leonie to the car park.'

'No need,' she said swiftly, taking the keys.

'I insist,' he said suavely. He bowed to Jess, then escorted Leonie through the foyer and out into the brightly lit car park. She hurried towards her sister's car, desperate to put an end to the uncomfortable interlude, not blaming Jess at all for avoiding the final, awkward leave-taking.

'I know it's pointless to make more apologies, so goodbye, Roberto,' she said unhappily, then gave a gasp of horror as a tall figure strolled casually towards them.

'Won't you introduce me to your friend, darling?' said Jonah.

'Yes, of course,' said Leonie, after a tense pause. 'Roberto, this is my fiancé, Jonah Savage. Jonah, this is Roberto Forli.'

'*Piacere,*' lied Roberto, since it was obvious that the last emotion he was feeling was pleasure.

'How do you do?' said Jonah, putting a possessive arm round Leonie's waist. 'I've heard a lot about you.'

Roberto gave her a startled glance, then smiled coldly. 'You have the advantage of me, Signor Savage. Until tonight I had no idea you existed.'

'Good heavens, you here, Jonah?' said Jess, hurrying to join them.

He stared at her in surprise. 'Yes. I came to drive Leo home. What are *you* doing here, Jess?'

'I flatly refused to stay at home, so I made Leonie bring me along,' she said flippantly, and smiled at Roberto. 'Thank you for putting up with an extra guest.'

'It was my great pleasure,' he assured her, and this time made it plain he actually meant it.

'I didn't know you were with Leo, so I came to take her home,' said Jonah. 'Would you mind driving back on your own, Jess?'

'Not in the least!' she assured him.

'Then if you are not returning with your sister, Miss Jessamy,' said Roberto smoothly, 'can I persuade you to stay awhile, and drink more coffee with me? It is early yet.'

Jess exchanged a mischievous look with Leonie, and held out her hand for the car keys. 'Why not? I'd like that very much. I'll see you two back at the ranch.'

Roberto took formal leave of Leonie and Jonah, then escorted Jess into the hotel, leaving a simmering silence behind them.

'It's been quite a day for surprises,' said Jonah at last,

and looked down into Leonie's face. 'I couldn't reach you on your cellphone.'

'It's out of juice, so I left it at home.'

'When I couldn't reach you I rang Friars Wood, but your father just said you'd gone into Pennington. He didn't say you'd taken Jess with you.'

'I thought you'd be pleased that I did,' she snapped, as they walked towards his car.

'Pleased? I'm delighted. I hated the thought of you dining alone with the man. And that was before I knew he looked like a bloody film star!' Jonah unlocked the car and helped her in. 'It was a great idea to bring Jess, darling.'

'It was her idea, not mine.'

Jonah slid in behind the wheel and turned to look at her. 'So you were determined to have your own way, no matter what I said?'

'Yes,' she said, seething. 'And a fat lot of good it did me.'

Jonah grinned suddenly. 'If the poor devil had Jess listening while you dumped him, I almost feel sympathy for him.'

'Do you indeed?' Leonie glared at him. 'Jess tactfully removed herself after dinner, of course, so I could talk to Roberto alone.'

'Ah. How did he take it?'

'Badly. He feels I've made a fool of him.' She stared angrily through the windscreen. 'I hate to admit it, Jonah, but I should have listened to you and stayed at home. The personal touch was a stupid mistake. Roberto, it seems, would have much preferred a phone call after all. So much for my high-flown principles.'

Jonah eyed her furious profile warily, then started the car. 'Let's go back to the lodge—'

'If you've got a repeat performance of last night in mind,' she snapped, 'I'm not in the mood.'

There was a very nasty pause.

'I was actually thinking of lighting the fire and just having a quiet drink in front of it to round off a damned exhausting day,' said Jonah coldly. 'But if that's the mood you're in I'll take you straight home.'

'No, please don't!' she said quickly, and gave him a penitent smile. 'Sorry. I've been in a foul mood all evening.'

'Why?'

'Because you didn't ring before I went out.'

He laughed, and put a hand on her knee. 'I missed you by minutes. I rang to give you my deeply reluctant blessing and offer to drive you home afterwards.'

'I wish I'd known. I was horrified when you appeared out of the blue like that,' she admitted.

'Why?'

'I didn't want you and Roberto to meet. I didn't even want him to come with me to the car, but he insisted.'

'Very right and proper, too!'

'So you're on his side now?'

'No, Leo. I'm not. In fact I'd quite like to drop the subject of Signor Forli. Let's go home and forget everyone in the world but the two of us for a while.'

Leonie was all for it, and sat as close to Jonah as she could all the way back to the lodge, beginning to relax at last as they left the tensions of the day behind.

When they arrived she made tea in the kitchen while Jonah set a match to the logs in the fireplace in his office, chuckling to herself as she investigated the box on the table.

'Can I have something to eat?' she called.

'Anything you like.' Jonah came in, grinning. 'My mother gives me a food parcel every time she sees me.'

'Good,' said Leonie with satisfaction. 'I fancy a sandwich.'

'You've just had dinner in the best restaurant for miles around, not to mention the wonderful lunch your mother gave us earlier on, and you're *still* hungry?'

'I didn't eat much either time. Tension is a very effective appetite depressant.' Leonie smiled at him seraphically. 'I'm not the least bit tense now.'

They made cheese and ham sandwiches, added some of Flora Savage's renowned coconut cake, then took a loaded tray into the other room.

'This,' said Leonie, with a sigh, 'is just what I need. Some nice plain food, a roaring fire, and just you and me together, Jonah.'

'My sentiments exactly,' he agreed. 'Do you know what really made me come after you tonight?'

'Jealousy?' she said hopefully.

'That, too. But it suddenly occurred to me that what Jess said about trust applied to me as much as to you. I rang you up to tell you that, but the bird had flown.' He grinned down at her. 'I couldn't quite bring myself to have you paged at the Chesterton. Knowing that temper of yours, you'd probably have told me to get lost before I could get a word in.'

Leonie opened her mouth to deny it, then laughed instead. 'I was in such a strop I might have done, at that.'

They finished their meal in perfect accord, idly discussing the when and where and how of their wedding.

'We can live in the flat to start with, and look for a house at our leisure,' he said musingly. 'Once I've got Brockhill up and running I shan't be needed much down here. Do you intend looking for a teaching post in London?'

Leonie stacked the tray with their used plates, then resumed her place on the sofa. 'It depends.'

'On what?' he asked, pulling her close.

'On whether we were successful last night.'

'Ah!' He turned her face up to his and kissed her gently.

Leonie smiled at him. 'Remember what I said in the car?'

'About what, in particular?' he enquired, his kiss rather less gentle as she wriggled closer.

'I said I wasn't in the mood.'

'So you did.'

'I've changed my mind.'

'That's a pity,' Jonah sighed. 'Because I don't think *I'm* in the mood now.'

Leonie stared up at him in utter dismay. 'Do you mean that?'

Jonah pretended to think about it. 'Well,' he said slyly, 'I suppose you could always try seducing me.'

'Oh, could I?' Leonie gave him a very unloverlike dig in the ribs. 'For a moment there I thought you were into revenge again.'

'No.' He smiled into her eyes. 'But I have a problem. Since you mentioned the seduction idea I can't get it out of my mind. And you've got a lot to make up to me, remember?'

She nodded demurely. 'You're right. I do. However, as I said before, I've never tried seducing anyone. But I'll do my best.'

Leonie's 'best' began with a slow, provocative strip-tease, and, as she warmed to the task, became so creative that in the end Jonah seized the initiative and embarked on a highly satisfactory seduction of his own.

'How about this wedding?' demanded Jonah later, when he could speak coherently.

'As soon as possible,' gasped Leonie, with unblushing fervour.

'You could move in with me until we actually tie the knot,' he suggested.

She smiled up at him coaxingly. 'Indulge me, Jonah. I'd rather live at home until we're actually married.'

'Of course I'll indulge you!' He sighed and held her close. 'I've been seven years without you, so I suppose I can exist a couple of weeks longer. What do you say to a special licence to speed things up?'

'Brilliant idea.' Leonie kissed him ardently. 'This sofa's all very well, darling, but I prefer the bed in your flat. Provided with a few home comforts, I fancy I could do a lot better at this seduction thing!'

VIVA LA VIDA DE AMOR!

They speak the language of passion.

In Harlequin Presents®, you'll find a special kind of lover—full of Latin charm. Whether he's relaxing in denims or dressed for dinner, giving you diamonds or simply sweet dreams, he's got spirit, style and sex appeal!

Latin Lovers is the new miniseries from Harlequin Presents® for anyone who enjoys hot romance!

Meet gorgeous Antonio Scarlatti in
THE BLACKMAILED BRIDEGROOM
by Miranda Lee, Harlequin Presents® #2151
available January 2001

And don't miss sexy Niccolo Dominici in
THE ITALIAN GROOM
by Jane Porter, Harlequin Presents® #2168
available March 2001!

Available wherever Harlequin books are sold.

HARLEQUIN®
Makes any time special ™

He's a man of cool sophistication.
He's got pride, power and wealth.
He's a ruthless businessman, an expert lover—
and he's one hundred percent committed
to staying single.

Until now. Because suddenly he's responsible
for a BABY!

HIS BABY

An exciting miniseries from Harlequin Presents®
He's sexy, he's successful...
and now he's facing up to fatherhood!

On sale February 2001:
RAFAEL'S LOVE-CHILD
by Kate Walker, Harlequin Presents® #2160

On sale May 2001:
MORGAN'S SECRET SON
by Sara Wood, Harlequin Presents® #2180

And look out for more later in the year!

Available wherever Harlequin books are sold.

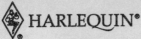

**Getting down
to business in
the boardroom…
and the bedroom!**

A secret romance, a forbidden affair,
a thrilling attraction…

What happens when two people work
together and simply can't help falling in
love—no matter how hard they try to resist?

Find out in our new series of stories set
against working backgrounds.

Look out for

THE MISTRESS CONTRACT
by Helen Brooks, Harlequin Presents® #2153
Available January 2001

and don't miss

SEDUCED BY THE BOSS
by Sharon Kendrick, Harlequin Presents® #2173
Available April 2001

Available wherever Harlequin books are sold.

HARLEQUIN®
Makes any time special ™

Visit us at www.eHarlequin.com   HP925

If you enjoyed what you just read,
then we've got an offer you can't resist!

Take 2 bestselling
love stories FREE!

Plus get a FREE surprise gift!

Clip this page and mail it to Harlequin Reader Service®

IN U.S.A.
3010 Walden Ave.
P.O. Box 1867
Buffalo, N.Y. 14240-1867

IN CANADA
P.O. Box 609
Fort Erie, Ontario
L2A 5X3

YES! Please send me 2 free Harlequin Presents® novels and my free surprise gift. Then send me 6 brand-new novels every month, which I will receive months before they're available in stores. In the U.S.A., bill me at the bargain price of $3.34 plus 25¢ delivery per book and applicable sales tax, if any*. In Canada, bill me at the bargain price of $3.74 plus 25¢ delivery per book and applicable taxes**. That's the complete price and a savings of at least 10% off the cover prices—what a great deal! I understand that accepting the 2 free books and gift places me under no obligation ever to buy any books. I can always return a shipment and cancel at any time. Even if I never buy another book from Harlequin, the 2 free books and gift are mine to keep forever. So why not take us up on our invitation. You'll be glad you did!

106 HEN C22Q
306 HEN C22R

Name	(PLEASE PRINT)	
Address	Apt.#	
City	State/Prov.	Zip/Postal Code

* Terms and prices subject to change without notice. Sales tax applicable in N.Y.
** Canadian residents will be charged applicable provincial taxes and GST.
   All orders subject to approval. Offer limited to one per household.
   ® are registered trademarks of Harlequin Enterprises Limited.

PRES00   ©1998 Harlequin Enterprises Limited

Lindsay Armstrong...
Helen Bianchin...
Emma Darcy...
Miranda Lee...

Some of our bestselling writers are Australians!

Look our for their novels about the Wonder from Down Under—where spirited women win the hearts of Australia's most eligible men.

THE **AUSTRALIANS**

Coming soon:

THE MARRIAGE RISK
by Emma Darcy
On sale February 2001, Harlequin Presents® #2157

And look out for:

MARRIAGE AT A PRICE
by Miranda Lee
On sale June 2001, Harlequin Presents® #2181

Available wherever Harlequin books are sold.

HARLEQUIN®
Makes any time special ™